"You really do like playing with fire, don't you?"

His mouth was inching toward hers. "How badly are you going to get burned before you learn your lesson?"

She could feel the warm draft of his breath against her mouth. Knew in advance how his lips would taste. A painful, grinding hunger consumed her, one she'd have sold her soul to satisfy.

"I don't know," she whispered recklessly. "Why don't you teach me?"

BRIDES OF CONVENIENCE

Forced into marriage—by a millionaire!

Four women demanded for marriage...
by four very sexy men who get everything
they want. And what they want is their new
wives in the bedroom.

Read all four wedding stories in this
new collection by your favorite authors,
available in Promotional Presents May 2007:

The Lawyer's Contract Marriage—
Amanda Browning

A Convenient Wife—
Sara Wood

The Italian's Virgin Bride—
Trish Morey

The Mediterranean Husband—
Catherine Spencer

THE MEDITERRANEAN HUSBAND

CATHERINE SPENCER

BRIDES OF CONVENIENCE

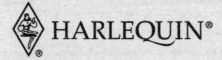

HARLEQUIN®

TORONTO • NEW YORK • LONDON
AMSTERDAM • PARIS • SYDNEY • HAMBURG
STOCKHOLM • ATHENS • TOKYO • MILAN • MADRID
PRAGUE • WARSAW • BUDAPEST • AUCKLAND

ISBN-13: 978-0-373-82052-8
ISBN-10:   0-373-82052-6

THE MEDITERRANEAN HUSBAND

First North American Publication 2007.

Copyright © 2006 by Spencer Books Limited.

This edition published by arrangement with Harlequin Books S.A.

® and TM are trademarks of the publisher. Trademarks indicated with ® are registered in the United States Patent and Trademark Office, the Canadian Trade Marks Office and in other countries.

www.eHarlequin.com

Printed in U.S.A.

THE MEDITERRANEAN HUSBAND

CHAPTER ONE

FROM his post on the roof, Demetrio had a clear view of the chauffeur-driven car as it eased its way to a stop under the portico of the villa next door. Sleek and powerful, the Mercedes reflected the woman who owned it.

Barbara Wade was a legend in the world of international business—a freak, according to some. Nearing sixty, she'd broken with tradition early, aspiring to become more than a diamond-draped accessory content to take a backseat to her successful husband—or, in Signora Wade's case, *husbands*. From what he'd gathered through *Forbes Magazine*, *Fortune 500* and similar publications, she'd frightened off the first two, and left the third in his grave.

That morning, though, it was not Barbara Wade who stepped out of the car, but a woman barely out of girlhood. Leggy and elegantly thin, with porcelain skin and brown hair falling glossy and straight to her shoulders, she had *American princess* written all over her. The granddaughter, he surmised. He'd heard the next-door gardeners talking among themselves that she was expected.

As though sensing she was being watched, she paused midway between the car and the front door of the villa and, lifting her head, met his gaze head-on. He knew what any common laborer would have done, caught acting so brazenly in that affluent strip of Italian real estate between Positano and Amalfi: look away and pretend he was observing the view. But Demetrio Bertoluzzi prided himself on being uncommon, and continued to stare.

What he knew to be no more than a well-ingrained stubborn streak coupled with injured pride on his part, *she* interpreted as outright impudence. It showed in the affronted tilt of her head, the subtle stiffening of her spine. Sweat-soaked Italian workmen, stripped to the waist and swinging a mason's hammer in one hand, did not openly feast their eyes on the cream of feminine American society, not if they wanted to keep their jobs.

What she didn't know, of course, was that he answered to no one. His own boss, he was free to stare all day, if he pleased. Nor was that all.

Amused, he allowed himself a small smile. How much more insulted she'd be, when she learned the rest. He could hear it now:

That man next door, Grandmother—who is he?

Oh, a very unsavory character, darling girl! Not at all the kind of man you want to know!

He was willing to guarantee she'd known very few men at all. Certainly had never had a man's hands discover her lily-white body. She exuded an aura too passionless, too untouchable. Too untouched.

Almost directly overhead, the late June sun glared down from a cloudless sky. Below, the blue Tyrhennian Sea spread all the way to Sicily. Perched between the two, on the lip of the steep cliff, lay the Villa Delfina, named for his late grandmother. *His* villa, now.

Stooping, he picked up the bottle of water leaning in the shade of one of the chimneys, and held it to his lips without once taking his eyes off the girl. Defeated, she finally dropped her gaze from him to the villa's roof, and from there to its faded stucco walls and dusty windows.

He knew what she saw. Almost fourteen years the house had stood empty and neglected, and over nine since his grandfather, Ovidio Bertoluzzi, had died in prison. A fitting end to a man whom his underworld associates had both feared and detested, and whom decent society had scorned.

At first, Demetrio had wanted no part of anything Ovidio had touched—and he'd left his stamp ingrained in the very walls of the villa. Even in death, his cold, hard eyes and chilling voice filled every room. Only when he realized he was letting the old man control him from beyond the grave did Demetrio allow expedience to prevail over pride, and agree to accept part of his inheritance.

But not the house on the Amalfi coast. The memories were too painful, the wounds still too raw. It had taken years before he'd been able to face it again, and even now he might never have returned, if it hadn't been for his grandmother.

The villa and its gardens had been her refuge. She had loved it—and she'd loved Demetrio. She'd been the only person who had, and it was out of respect and love for her that he'd eventually come back to claim it as his own. It would have broken her heart to see the desecration inflicted by vandals; the damage caused by weather, rodents, time.

The American princess had turned away, no doubt horrified by what she'd found next door. Vandalism didn't occur in villas perched along the Amalfi coast—unless those houses happened once to have belonged to mobsters. Then, of course, they became fair game for anyone with mischief in mind, and the authorities were only too happy to look the other way. Whatever it took to rid the area of human vermin was okay by them.

His smile disappeared, swiped away by his forearm as he

drew it across his mouth. "But I'm not vermin and I'm not going anywhere, princess," he said softly, "so better get used to it."

"I thought I heard the car! Darling, why on earth are you standing out here in this blistering heat when I have cool drinks waiting on the terrace?" Splendid in a bronze silk caftan that whispered expensively around her ankles, her grandmother swept down the steps and folded Natalie in a scented hug.

As well as exquisite designer clothes, and bold, one-of-a-kind jewelry, Barbara Wade favored *Diva* perfume, surely the only appropriate fragrance for a woman who claimed center stage, no matter who else might be present. Outspoken, aggressive and glamorous, she was a force to be reckoned with on any level. But if she had a head for business that left international tycoons eating her dust, she also had a heart whose limitless capacity for love had been Natalie's lodestar for longer than she could remember.

Flinging her arms around her grandmother, Natalie said, "You don't know how glad I am that I decided to spend the summer here! You never change, and I'm so grateful for that."

Her grandmother held her at arm's length and observed her closely. "I heard about Lewis, my darling. Are you very crushed?"

Natalie laughed. "No woman likes to be dumped, but he was never the great love of my life. Honestly, Grandmother, I was about to end it between us, myself. He just happened to beat me to it, is all."

"Your mother thought you'd marry him."

"My mother *hoped* I'd marry him and forget about a career with Wade International. There's a difference."

"Yes, I suppose there is." Her grandmother subjected her to another searching scrutiny. "Is that why you're looking a little out of sorts? Because you've had a run-in with my daughter?"

"No." Natalie cast another glance at the roof of the building next door. *He* was still up there, lounging against the chimney stack, and staring insolently. A dangerous man on a dangerous mission.

An involuntary shiver chased over her. Where had that thought come from? And why was her skin puckering, and warning bells clanging in her mind?

Curious to discover what had caught her attention, her grandmother looked up also and clicked her tongue in annoyance. "The neighborhood's gone to the dogs, I'm afraid," she declared brusquely, ushering Natalie inside the villa and away from that disconcertingly bold gaze. "I'd hoped that place would be put back on the market and sold to someone respectable, but it appears not to be the case."

Despite herself, Natalie couldn't resist one last look over her shoulder. "You mean, that man *owns* the place?"

"Unfortunately he does, darling. But don't concern yourself. He's not welcome in this neighborhood, and he knows better than to impose himself on us."

But he'd already imposed himself on Natalie. Albeit from a distance, his brazen stare had seemed to penetrate her linen jacket and skirt, and see right through to the skin and bones they concealed. She'd felt nakedly, disturbingly exposed, and not just physically. Somehow, he'd probed clean through to her inner self and invaded the secret part of her—the hopes, the dreams that she shared with no one.

"Why do you say he's not respectable?" she asked, following her grandmother across the foyer's cool marble floor.

"He's a Bertoluzzi, hopefully the last of a bad lot. They came from Crotone originally, where they were known—and feared!—for their involvement in organized crime. Would you believe his father was killed by a rival gang leader, who himself turned up dead as a doornail in a meat locker a few days later? But what else can you expect from people whose entire lives revolve around mayhem and murder?"

Fans whirled lazily from the high ceiling. A sparkling crystal chandelier hung in the well formed by the curving staircase. Huge porcelain jardinieres imported from China overflowed with flowers picked fresh from the garden that morning.

Natalie knew there'd be a bouquet in her room, too, and on the bed, cotton sheets scented with lavender and ironed to a fare-thee-well. She'd find hand-milled French soap in her bathroom, thick, velvety towels, custom-blended body lotions.

The protocol for household staff remained the same, no matter which of her many luxury residences Barbara Wade happened to call home at the time. She could afford the very best, and never settled for less.

Yet here she was, practically rubbing shoulders with a neighbor whose connections were, to say the least, dubious.

Intrigued, Natalie said, "How long has the family lived here?"

"Over twenty-five years. The present owner's grandfather bought the place."

"Even at that time, it must have cost a small fortune. How could he afford it?"

Her grandmother rolled her eyes in disgust. "Extortion of some kind, probably! One thing you can be sure of, he paid for it with dirty money."

"I'm surprised the Residents' Association approved the sale."

"They wouldn't have, if they'd known. But the entire transaction was conducted in such an abominably underhanded manner by a local property dealer who, sadly, is still up to his neck in shady deals in the area, that those of us already living here had no idea who the new owners were until it was a fait accompli. If we had, we'd have moved heaven and earth to block the sale. But times have changed since his grandfather's day, and *no one* is about to let young Mr. Bertoluzzi get away with anything the least bit suspect. He puts one foot on the wrong side of the law, and he'll wish he'd never shown his face here again."

On that note, her grandmother brushed her hands together and swept aside the subject of the infamous family next door. "Romero will be serving the midday meal shortly, and I haven't had my prelunch vodka tonic yet. Will you join me, darling, or do you prefer a glass of wine?"

"I'll stick with wine, please," Natalie responded, keeping pace with her grandmother as she strode briskly through the house to the big, shaded patio overlooking the coast.

No matter how often she visited Villa Rosamunda, that first glance out at the sweeping spread of sea and sky always took Natalie's breath away. Because of the steep terrain, the garden fell away in a series of terraces, leaving an observer with an unobstructed view extending from the town of Amalfi to the east, as far as Positano to the west.

On the upper terrace, the largest by far, hibiscus bushes in shades of peach, salmon and scarlet filled huge urns set at intervals around a swimming pool the color of blue topaz. Beyond the stone balustrade separating the pool area from the landscaped lower terraces, bougainvillea grew in a riot of purple and orange, while a grove of lemon trees marked the boundary between the garden proper and the neighbors on one side. The other place, which *he* owned, lay on the other.

More fascinated than she ought to have been by the revelation that her grandmother's pristine Mediterranean paradise had been tainted by organized crime, Natalie waited until their drinks had been served, then remarked casually, "You've owned this place a long time. How is it I've never heard you mention this Bertoluzzi family until now?"

"Because, as you might recall from previous visits, their house has stood empty for a number of years. Ovidio Bertoluzzi, the patriarch, ended up in prison, and his wife died not long after that. She was a rather charming, gentle soul, and quite a beauty in her day. One has to wonder whatever prompted her to marry a man like that, when there must have been plenty of others of decent background who'd have been happy to have her."

"Maybe she loved him," Natalie said.

Her grandmother's laughter brimmed with affectionate scorn. "What an incurable romantic you are, my darling! Not the best quality for a woman destined to head Wade International some day, but endearing, nonetheless."

"I don't see why the two can't mix. *You've* fallen in love enough to marry three times, after all, but you never let it hold you back."

"Romance and business can go together, I suppose, given the right combination of personalities. Unfortunately, men strong enough to cope with a hugely successful wife aren't easily come by. Most are afraid they'll wind up stripped of their masculinity."

"I think that's what frightened off Lewis."

"Then you're well rid of him."

"I know," Natalie said, and wondered why the thought immediately swimming to the forefront of her mind was that it would take a lot more than success to scare away the man next door.

Her grandmother touched her hand fondly. "How are things at home otherwise, Natalie? Do you spend much time there?"

"Not as much as my father would like. He doesn't understand why, with what he calls 'all this modern technology paraphernalia,' I can't deal with the Boston office long-distance, and work out of the house."

"That's because he's able to see no farther than the end of a golf club or his yacht. It's just as well he married into money."

"That's not what keeps him and Mother together. They love each other dearly." Barbara had never appreciated her son-in-law's mild and gentle nature, and she never would. Knowing it to be something on which she and her grand-mother had long ago agreed to disagree, Natalie dropped the subject and returned to the vastly more interesting topic of Mr. Bertoluzzi. "So, I gather you were surprised when you found you had a next-door neighbor again?"

"'Appalled' more aptly describes my reaction! The place had stood abandoned for so long that I think everyone around here hoped it would just quietly crumble into dust, and that would be the end of it *and* the Bertoluzzis. Then, one morning out of the blue, the rusty old gates clanged open and there was the grandson, driving a truck crammed with tools and building supplies. We haven't known a truly peaceful day since. He's hammering or running power tools from dawn to dusk."

"Maybe he's fixing the place up in order to sell it."

Her grandmother downed the last of her vodka tonic and held out the glass to Romero for a refill. "One can only hope, darling! One can only hope!"

As usually happened after the long transatlantic flight, Natalie's body clock was off-kilter, and although she went to bed shortly after dinner that night, she found herself wide-awake again just after one in the morning. When not even the rhythmic swish and murmur of the sea could lull her back to sleep, she threw back the bedcovers and stepped out to the balcony running the width of her room.

How bright and near the stars appeared. Big, splashy diamonds hanging just out of reach in the navy sky, they patterned the sea with shifting sparks of light. No wonder her grandmother spent most summers here.

Natalie leaned against the balcony railing and, as her vision adjusted to the night, the garden below swam into more distinct definition. The water in the pool rolled gently like a length of satin buoyed by just the faintest puff of breeze. Dense black foliage framed the pale globes of the blossoms lining the flower beds. The lawns assumed a palette of subdued gray.

Close by her feet, the newly opened bud from a climbing rose poked through the veranda's wrought-iron railing, dark as blood. Stooping, she inhaled the delicate fragrance, then lifted her head sharply as another scent, smokily aromatic, teased her senses.

It came from the other side of the wall to the east, floating on the air in a faint cloud. Citronella, to ward off night-flying insects, she realized, and rising on tiptoe, detected the glimmer of a candle set in a hurricane lantern on the outer wall of an upstairs balcony next door.

A movement just to the left of it caught her eye. The Bertoluzzi man lounged with one hip perched on the loggia wall, and she wondered how she'd missed noticing him before. A lamp somewhere deep in the room behind him cast a dim glow, leaving his face shadowed and his white T-shirt shining ghostlike in the gloom.

As she watched, he raised a glass high and held it motionless a moment in a silent toast, then lowered it to his mouth and drank. There was something so languidly insolent in his every movement that she knew he'd seen her, long before she'd been aware of him; that he'd been watching her from the second she'd stepped out on the balcony.

Her first instinct was to slink back into her room and hide behind the filmy drapes. But pride held her in place. Painfully conscious though she was of wearing next to nothing, she refused to betray her discomfiture by hunching her shoulders, crossing her arms over her chest and shrinking out of sight. Instead, with the blood suddenly pumping furiously through her veins, she faced him defiantly.

What he was like, up close? she wondered, both repelled and fascinated by him. She didn't need her grandmother's recital of his family's shortcomings to warn her that if she had a grain of sense, she'd keep well clear of him. His alien aura of bold masculinity made him unlike other men she knew—the country club types and political appointees who, should they ever find it necessary to dabble in questionable business, would hire a front man to deal with it before they'd soil their own hands.

Not Bertoluzzi, though. If there was dirty work to be done, she had no doubt he'd take care of it himself.

What was his first name? How old was he? Did he have a wife? A girlfriend?

Not the latter, she decided. A girlfriend was too innocuous for a man like him. More likely a mistress, another man's wife, probably.

She could envision some poor deluded creature being seduced by his brazen stare. No doubt he was an accomplished lover. He had that look about him—the kind that left a woman bathed in heat and shockingly aware of her sexuality. He'd have no trouble convincing a wife to break her wedding vows for a stolen night or two with him.

Aghast to find herself eaten up with a curiosity that left her nipples thrusting against the thin stuff of her nightgown, and a sweet foreign ache invading the pit of her stomach, Natalie decided to put an end to the present situation before she embarrassed herself further.

Not quite soon enough, however. Even as she went to avert her gaze, he stepped away from the balcony wall, lithe as some jungle animal and, she was sure, just as lethal. Tossing back the remains of his drink, he sauntered toward the open French doors behind him, then paused to face her one last time and lift his hand in a salute.

An unmistakably amused, *try-to-get-a grip* kind of salute, as if, *again,* he'd known exactly the thoughts filling her mind!

Pride deserted her then. Cheeks flaming, she spun around and scuttled into her room like the frightened rabbit she surely must be.

She couldn't be sure, but she thought, as she slid her own French doors shut, that she heard his distant laughter floating on the night air.

CHAPTER TWO

DID she really take the wrong path back from the beach by accident, four days later? Or was it a deliberate oversight on her part because persistent curiosity eventually got the better of discretion?

Whatever the true reason, once Natalie embarked on her course, there was no turning back. The climb up the cliff was too grueling. Unfortunately, by the time she reached the top and struggled over the vine-covered wall into the unkempt garden next door, curiosity had given way to a pathetic attack of cowardice.

Luck was on her side, though. There was no sign of *him* and, judging by the relentless whine of an electric saw somewhere on the far side of the house, he was too busy to realize his privacy had been invaded.

Not only that, escape lay within easy reach. A line of overgrown shrubbery protected her from view. She could have ducked behind it and been down the driveway, through the front gates and out on the road in a matter of minutes, with him none the wiser—if she'd exercised a grain of common sense.

But it, like discretion, proved to be in short supply that morning, and just as *he* held an incomprehensible fascination for her, so did his property. She'd lived in luxury all her life.

Grown up in a prime waterfront mansion in Talbot County, on Maryland's Easter Shore, attended by devoted nannies and servants. Had, in the course of her international travels, visited royal palaces and other landmarks whose architecture and rich appointments were legendary.

Notwithstanding all that, she remained inexplicably drawn to the sight greeting her now. The run-down Bertoluzzi villa, drowsing in the sun, held a mystique, a certain faded dignity, that refused to go ignored.

She had no earthly excuse for crossing to the open door on the far side of a sun-splashed patio. And, of course, absolutely no right to peep inside. But knowing this intellectually did nothing to deter her. It merely whetted her curiosity further.

In less time than it took for another drop of water to drip from the rusty pipe sticking out of what must once have been a gargoyle wall fountain, she was over the threshold and into a vast kitchen of sorts.

Terra-cotta tiles, broken in places and missing entirely in others, covered the floor. An old sink stood under the window, with a slab of marble cantilevered at a perilous angle from the wall next to it. An outdated refrigerator clanked in one corner.

In the middle of the room, a sheet of plywood, propped up on two sawhorses, served as a rough table which held a pottery mug, an empty mineral water bottle, and a portable two-burner stove connected to the nearest electrical outlet by a long extension cord.

Unpleasantly sticky from the heat, and so thirsty her tongue was practically sticking to the roof of her mouth, Natalie dropped her beach bag and sunglasses on the table, and wondered if the villa's water supply was safe to drink. Probably not, given the rusty stain in the sink and the fact that *he* obviously drank bottled water. The latter being so, logic suggested he probably kept a supply on hand and it didn't take mental genius to figure out where.

She pulled open the refrigerator door, and found a dozen or more bottles of mineral water, as well as enough beer to keep an army of ten supplied for a week. Without a moment's hesitation, she helped herself to a bottle of water.

She'd been brought up to be scrupulously honest, and normally would have been appalled to find herself stealing. But she was behaving nothing like her normal self that day, perhaps, she thought dizzily, because dehydration had rendered her slightly mad. What other reason accounted for her prowling around a stranger's house as if it were her own? But at that moment, quenching her thirst took priority over all else. She'd worry about social correctness later. Tipping back her head, she gulped down half the water before continuing her exploration of the room.

A man's shirt hung from a nail driven into the wall. Denim cotton, worn to the softness of silk by frequent washings, she decided, fingering the fabric. No evidence of a woman's presence, though. Did he take care of his own laundry? Cook his own meals on the little two-burner stove?

"The villa's not up to much, but the land's worth a small fortune," Barbara had declared at dinner the other evening. "Why the man doesn't cash in on the real estate market and move on, instead of picking away at repairing something that isn't worth saving, heaven only knows. If he sold the place, he could live comfortably on the proceeds for the rest of his life—somewhere far from here, of course!"

Her grandmother made a valid point. Properties such as this, with its sprawling grounds and million-dollar view, would attract buyers like bees to a honeypot. When he could live in comfort somewhere else, why a man with neither wife nor children to worry about would tackle restoring to its original grandeur a house large enough to accommodate a sizable family, made no apparent sense.

Wandering to the back door again, Natalie gazed out. Roses run wild tangled with bougainvillea and some other kind of vine she couldn't name. Butterflies flitted over brilliantly colored flower beds choked with weeds. What might once have been manicured lawns had deteriorated into long fragrant grass that spilled over the ancient slabs of stone pathways.

Birdsong filled the air, accompanied by the soothing murmur of a waterfall trickling down a wall of natural rock into a swimming pool spanned by a bridge. Although the rest of the garden had not been tended in years, the pool sparkled and was clearly in use.

Why didn't he just move on? She knew why!

Even in its present run-down state, this would be a very difficult place to leave. It possessed a timeless serenity. An ambience that had nothing to do with crime, but spoke of contentment. Of passions soaked in romance, not blood.

People had lived and loved here, long before the Bertoluzzis had moved in. It had known a baby's first cry, children's laughter, whispered endearments between a man and a woman in love.

"What would you say, if you could speak?" she murmured, laying the flat of her hand against the sun-warmed doorjamb.

"I imagine," a voice as dark and exotic as a tropical night drawled from somewhere deep in the room behind her, "that the first thing would be, what the hell do you think you're doing, inviting yourself in and making yourself at home here?"

She spun around, so full of startled guilt that the water bottle flew out of her hand and shattered on the terra-cotta tile. All loose-limbed, relaxed strength, Bertoluzzi leaned in the doorway leading from the kitchen to the remainder of the house, one thumb hooked negligently into a belt loop, but she had not the slightest doubt that if she tried to make a run for it, he'd be across the room and catch her before she so much as cleared the threshold at the back door.

A pair of faded blue jeans clung to his lean hips. The expanse of smooth muscled flesh above them, tanned to a perfect bronze, made her mouth run dry all over again.

Trying to ignore the fact that he was again stripped to the waist and that, up this close, he had the kind of body that would make the most rabid feminist reconsider the wisdom of shunning all that was masculine and beautiful, she looked him in the face again.

Sculpted cheekbones, strong jaw, sensuous mouth, unswerving gaze, unreadable expression... The clichés tripped over themselves in her mind, every one true.

Devil or angel? Both, she decided, with his mood determining which reigned supreme in any given situation.

Just then, the devil had the upper hand. "Well? Let's hear it."

"I'm so sorry!" she stammered. "I took the wrong path up from the beach and found myself in your garden."

"But you're not in my garden," he pointed out lazily. "You're in my house, drinking my water and making one hell of a mess while you're at it."

"I know." She scanned the room, willing a broom to appear out of thin air, to no effect. "Of course, I'll clean it up."

"It goes without saying that you will. And while you're at it, I suggest you also come up with a more plausible explanation for your uninvited presence. Even if it's true that you followed the wrong path from the beach—" his pause made it clear he believed no such thing "—you can hardly expect me to buy that once you reached my property, you mistook it for your grandmother's pristine estate next door."

"How do you know she's my grandmother?"

He advanced farther into the kitchen, an infinitesimal smile touching a mouth that was anything but amused. "There's very little that goes on around here that I'm not aware of."

He's a Bertoluzzi...his father was murdered by a rival crime boss...

Despite the sun streaming through the door to bathe the kitchen in warmth, a chill raced up Natalie's spine at the recollection of her grandmother's words.

He'd caught her trespassing in his house, no one else knew she was there, and even if she'd been able to force a scream from her beleaguered lungs, no one would have heard her.

Not about to let him know that he scared her witless, she said loftily, "I'm sure there isn't. You made no secret of your interest in my arrival at my grandmother's, the other day. Tell me, do you spend a great deal of time spying on your neighbors, or was it just dumb luck that you happened to notice when I got here?"

"I don't believe in luck, dumb or otherwise, any more than I believe you strolled into my house by mistake. So tell me, princess, why are you really here? And this time, try sticking to the truth."

He was a big, powerful man, in his early to mid-thirties she guessed, with the tough build of a laborer. His black hair, cut short to tame its natural curl, gleamed with sweat, as did his darkly tanned skin. But the feature that struck her most forcibly were his eyes. A piercing, unusually light blue, they made an arresting statement in an already unforgettable face.

To label him "handsome" was too bland a description. On the other hand, "sultry," "sexy," "passionate" and "dangerous" might have been created with him in mind.

"Cat got your tongue, princess? Or are you suddenly remembering that Grandmama warned you not to speak to types like me?"

Types like him? Ye gods, she'd never before come across *anyone* remotely like him! Never been confronted by such simmering animal magnetism. As for the withering scorn in his remarkable eyes...

"I don't think I like your tone or your attitude," she declared, trying for haughty disdain, but afraid she managed nothing more than breathless titillation.

He looked away and laughed—sort of. "If you're so all-fired well brought up, how come no one taught you it's rude to stare?"

She blushed and dragged her gaze away from his impressive torso. "I wasn't."

"Sure you were."

He dismissed her lie with a careless shrug, then ambled to the sink and stuck his head under the tap. After a gurgle of protest, water gushed out to sluice over his hair and run down his shoulders.

Unable to help herself, she watched his every move as he raked back his hair. Water dripped from his chin, formed a rivulet down his chest, and disappeared inside the waist of his dusty blue jeans. He was more man than she'd ever met before—and, physically at least, certainly more man than she'd ever beheld with such unadorned, palpitating admiration.

Once, after she'd joined Lewis for dinner at his place, he'd caught her as she went to sit on the couch and pressing her up against the wall, said, "Why don't we take this into the bedroom, honey? It's about time, don't you think?"

She'd turned her head aside and shoved him away. "I don't think so!"

Hurt by her rejection, and probably feeling foolish, he'd let her go and asked sulkily, "Why not? Who are you saving yourself for, Natalie?"

Not you! her quelling glare had intimated, and mumbling an apology, he'd offered to drive her home.

But suddenly his question resurfaced. Who *was* she saving herself for?

The answer fell into place with such shocking certainty that she choked back a gasp, and ran her hand inside her low-cut top in a futile effort to stem the heat rising up her neck.

A man like you, Mr. Bertoluzzi!

She'd heard nothing good about him, but her first instinct held true. He'd be an expert lover. There'd be nothing clumsy about his moves. He'd never have to apologize and nor, she suspected, would any woman ever want him to.

Was that why her romance with Lewis had fizzled and died before it had ever bloomed? Because it was rooted in convenience? Was too bloodless, too lacking in passion ever to catch fire?

Or was it simply that she had too much sun this morning, and lost her mind completely?

Her glance slid again to the Italian's face and she realized that he was watching her. Those dramatic, unnerving blue eyes were scouring her face and correctly reading its every expression.

Then, bold as brass, his gaze slid down her body to her thighs, as if he knew they were trembling. As if he knew the flesh between them was hot and damp and aching.

Weak at the knees, she clutched the doorjamb again. Good grief, what was happening to her? Where was her sanity, that a single glance from a man like him could sear her so intimately that she was ready to give herself to him?

Wrenching her fast-disappearing dignity back in place, she said stiffly, "I realize I owe you an apology. Just for the record, I no more approve of illegal entry and theft than I do of murder."

He raised his eyebrows and studied the ceiling. "An interesting comparison," he drawled. "You're acquainted with the latter, are you?"

"No," she said. "Are you?"

So much for dignity! Like a pea about to choke her, the question had shot out of her mouth, and no amount of mumbling or stammering could suck it back in again. Horrified, she clapped a hand to her lips and froze. Why had she even mentioned the word "murder," let alone suggested he might engage in it?

He glanced aside, but not before she saw him struggling to keep the corners of his mouth from turning up. "What do you think, princess?"

"That I've prevailed on your hospitality long enough." She licked her parched lips. "Um…do you have something I can use to clean up the mess I've made?"

Shaking his head, he disappeared through the door from which he'd first appeared, and was back a moment later with a broom and dustpan. She took them, careful not to let her fingers touch his, and set about sweeping up the broken bottle.

She was far too rattled to make a good job of it. For every chunk of glass she retrieved and shoveled onto the dustpan, three more slithered off. As for the smaller pieces, they lodged in the cracks between the floor tiles and refused to budge, no matter how industriously she attacked them. And all the time, he trained those piercing blue eyes on her and said not a word.

She wished she was wearing a skirt that fell to her ankles, a long-sleeved blouse that buttoned up to the throat. Better yet, a nun's habit. Anything but the short shorts and sleeveless tank top which had seemed perfectly suitable when she'd put them on that morning, and which now struck a glaringly inappropriate note.

Flustered by his unremitting gaze, and increasingly embarrassed by her own ineptitude, she muttered, "What must you think of me?"

His gaze cruised indolently from her feet to her flushed face, and that secretive little smile flitted over his mouth again. "*Signorina,* you don't want to know!"

The innuendo in his reply was unmistakable. If he'd approached her and drawn his finger from her throat to the juncture of her thighs, she couldn't have been more shaken. Even worse, he sensed it and, his smile broadening, he advanced toward her.

Trembling, she swallowed a breath and at the last minute, shut her eyes. She didn't want to see what might happen next, be it a stolen kiss, a forbidden caress, or however else he chose to close in for the kill. She just wanted to survive it.

Kill. The literal implications of the word echoed through the chambers of her mind. Her grandmother had warned her about this man. Why hadn't she listened?

Helpless, she stood at his mercy. Heard his measured footsteps approach across the terra-cotta tiles. Felt the heat of his skin, inhaled its scent: sweat and sunshine and sawdust. And then she felt his touch. Strong, callused hands on hers. And his breath drifting warmly over her face.

"I suggest," he murmured, relieving her of the broom and dustpan, "that you remove yourself…before you get a speck of dirt on those nice clean shorts."

She grabbed her bag and sunglasses, and bolted from the room and down the rutted driveway to the road as if the hounds of hell were in pursuit. Clearly she believed him to be only one notch above the devil incarnate, something for which he no doubt had her grandmother to thank.

Not surprising. He'd known all along that, as far as the neighbors were concerned, he was a blight on the face of decent society. The sins of the father—and in his case, grandfather and several generations before that—weren't easily forgotten.

Still, he should be ashamed of himself, frightening her like that. Her eyes had grown huge in her face when he'd approached her, the pupils dilated with such shocked apprehension that he'd thought she might faint.

For a moment, he'd felt sorry enough for her to want to take hold of her trembling shoulders and reassure her that he meant her no harm. Just as well he hadn't done so. He'd have had to be brain-dead not to notice what a beauty she was. A true thoroughbred, all fine, elegant bones, clear creamy skin and polished hair.

Laying a hand on her, even for humanitarian reasons would, if word ever got out, have been asking for nothing but trouble he didn't need. He hadn't come back to Villa Delfina to blacken further the already tarnished reputation he'd inherited. He'd come to prove the point that a man deserved to be judged on his own merits, not those of his ancestors, and becoming entangled with her was no way to go about it.

Still and all, getting rid of her physical presence was a lot easier than dismissing her from his mind. All afternoon, when he should have been concentrating on the delicate business of shoring up the underpinnings of the front steps, his thoughts kept veering back to her and the real reason behind her visit.

That she'd taken the wrong path was such a transparent lie, it was laughable. More likely, she'd wanted to see what a man like him—big, bad, and dangerous—looked like up close. She just hadn't figured on getting caught doing it, or on his getting too close for comfort. For all her haughty attitude and designer sunglasses, nothing she did or wore could hide the innocence in her heart.

It was that innocence that captured his imagination—and also what put her off-limits. If a woman was what he wanted, there were plenty to be had who didn't come with her kind of price tag attached. She was too young, too naive, too refined. He might as well invite a lynch mob to his front door as take up with her. Good thing he was smart enough to send her packing before temptation got the better of him.

CHAPTER THREE

THAT night over dinner, Natalie said, "I paid a visit to your next-door neighbor today."

"The Brambillas?" Her grandmother glanced up, surprised. "I understood they were away this week."

"I'm talking about your other neighbor. Mr. Bertoluzzi."

If she'd announced she'd found a live snake mating with her broiled scampi, her grandmother couldn't have looked more thunderstruck. "Good heavens, child, what on earth possessed you?"

"He interests me."

"Al Capone interests *me,* but I hope, if he were alive today and moved in next door, I'd have the good sense to steer clear of him!"

After recovering from her undignified flight that morning, though, Natalie had taken time to mull over her encounter with the man next door, and come to the conclusion that if he was one-tenth as bad as he was made out to be, she'd given him ample opportunity to prove it. Since she'd escaped with only her pride a little bruised, she felt honor bound to defend him now.

"I hardly think Mr. Bertoluzzi's in the same category as Al Capone. From all I can determine, his only sin is that he won't move out of his house, and I can't say I blame him. I wouldn't give up that property, either, if it were mine."

Very deliberately, her grandmother laid down her fork, and fixed Natalie in the kind of stare that left errant Wade employees quivering in their boots. "He's not our kind of person, my dear, nor is he the kind embraced by anyone else in the area."

"How do you know that?"

Never one to suffer fools gladly, her grandmother shot her a look that made it clear what she thought of such a patently stupid question. "I already told you," she replied, enunciating each syllable with exaggerated patience. "It's an established fact that his family had connections to—"

"Organized crime. Yes, I haven't forgotten."

"And did you remember the rest—about his grandfather, his—?"

"Every word. But what's any of that got to do with him?"

"Well, *darling!*" Barbara's perfectly arched eyebrows rose another incredulous notch. "The apple seldom falls far from the tree."

"How can you say that, and keep a straight face? My mother's chief interest is meeting her cronies for lunch and keeping her appointment book up-to-date. As for my father, he doesn't know the difference between a bond and a debenture, and cares even less. But that's not stopping you from hoping their only child will step into your shoes as head of Wade International one day."

"Because we are different."

"No, we're not. We've got a closet full of family skeletons, too."

"Nothing like his, Natalie. Murder, extortion and incarceration play no part in our history."

"Great-grandfather Wade gambled."

"But he didn't cheat."

"Not that you know of. But he rarely walked away from the poker table a loser, and we're not talking penny ante stakes here. If facts are what you want to toss back and forth, it's a matter of record that his winnings often left other men's lives in ruins. Some people say that if he'd lived long enough, he'd have ended up with the whole of Talbot County real estate in his back pocket."

"He was a shrewd investor."

At that, Natalie couldn't contain a burst of disbelieving laughter. "Will you listen to yourself? He preyed on other men's weakness! He took away the roofs over their children's heads! One poor soul is rumored to have hanged himself because he lost everything playing poker with Edgar Wade."

"Those men were free to walk away from the table, anytime they chose. It's not your great-grandfather's fault they were fools."

"Exactly! And it's not Mr. Bertoluzzi's fault that his father and grandfather were criminals."

Barbara dabbed the corner of her mouth with her napkin and leaned across the table. "Listen, Natalie," she said earnestly. "There are families in this part of the country—honest, law-abiding families—who've suffered terribly because of the Bertoluzzis. Mothers who feared for their teenage daughters' innocence. Deals offered to husbands and fathers in a way that made it clear there were no choices about accepting, not if those men wanted to live their lives unafraid. Sons who disappeared without explanation, and were never again heard from. Houses that mysteriously burned down."

"That all happened a very long time ago, Grandmother."

"Yes, it did. But people still remember."

"Well, of course they do," Natalie said. "Who can forget

that sort of tragedy? But the last I heard, a man is innocent until proven guilty, and as far as I can tell, Mr. Bertoluzzi has done nothing to provoke suspicion. What's his first name, by the way? I find it ridiculous to keep referring to him as Mr."

"I'm not sure what he calls himself. Damiano, or something similar, and very fitting, too, if you ask me since he's certainly the spawn of the devil. And *I* find it ridiculous that we're even having this conversation."

"Ostracizing him won't make him go away."

"It might."

"No, Grandmother, not this man. He didn't strike me as someone who cares much about topping the popularity polls."

"Well, what about you, Natalie? Have you stopped to think how championing him affects your credibility as Wade International's future CEO?"

"Oh, please!" She threw up her hands in disgust. "I'm talking about being neighborly, not signing over a chunk of the company to him."

"Not everyone will see it that way. A number of my friends and neighbors here own interests in WI. You're still young and inexperienced, darling, but even you must recognize that undermining confidence among even a handful of shareholders can have far-reaching and damaging consequences. And that's exactly the risk you take, if you insist on pursuing a relationship with this man."

At that point, any suggestion of amusement on Natalie's part dissolved into outright annoyance. "I'm not *pursuing a relationship,* for heaven's sake! All I'm suggesting is…"

What, exactly? That they invite him over for morning coffee, once in a while? Exchange flower cuttings over the garden wall? Because if that was all she had in mind, why did she go hot all over at the mention of his name. For that matter, why mention his name at all?

Unable to come up with a reasonable answer, even to herself, Natalie snapped her mouth shut.

"Yes?" Barbara regarded her expectantly.

"Nothing." She shook her head, at a loss to understand her obsession with a man who showed not the slightest interest in her. "You're right. I guess I need to get out more."

Spurred by that realization, she spent the next week visiting Theresa Lambert, an old school friend, now a journalist living in Rome. Together, they attended a concert in the Colosseum and a lunch-hour show in the heart of the fashion district, and toured a recently opened art exhibit in Vatican City.

When Theresa had to work, Natalie browsed the shops and revisited her favorite tourist sites. Most evenings, they went out, usually with men from Theresa's huge circle of friends who wined and dined them in fine style, and had other women turning for a second look.

Well, why not? They were charming men. Handsome, immaculately turned-out, cultured, educated, and eminently suitable. But at the end of the day, not one left enough of an impression for Natalie to differentiate between him and the rest.

"Well?" her grandmother greeted her, on her return to Villa Rosamunda. "Did you have a good time?"

"Wonderful," she said, when in fact, she hadn't been able to get back to Amalfi soon enough.

"And?"

"And what?"

"Did you meet anyone interesting?"

"As a matter of fact, I did. Theresa's next-door neighbor is a charming old lady."

"You know very well I'm not interested in hearing about charming old ladies. You're toying with me, Natalie!"

"Yes," she said sunnily, the sudden discordant tone of an

electric saw from next door music to her ears. "I learned how from you, Grandmother. You've taught me well."

A few days later, she received a phone call from the owner of an art shop in Positano, informing her an antique print she'd ordered for her mother's birthday was framed and ready for pickup.

It was a beautiful morning, and rather than take one of the cars or have her grandmother's chauffeur drive her, she decided to walk the eight kilometers into town. The exercise would do her good. After a week of dining out in Rome, her clothes were fitting a little too snugly around the waist.

The other benefit, of course, was being able to avoid the busy corniche road and take the cliffside trail instead. Heavily planted with trees, it offered shade from the sun, peace and quiet, and a panorama of spectacular scenery.

By contrast, Positano was packed with tourists, but not even the crowds could diminish the charm of its pastel-colored villas tumbling down the hillside. After collecting her print, she visited a fashion boutique, tempted by its display of extravagant sun hats, and emerged with an airy, wide-brimmed creation adorned with a cluster of bright red poppies. By then ready to give her feet a rest and escape the midday heat, she strolled down to the waterfront and found a pretty outdoor restaurant serving lunch at tables shaded by dark blue sun umbrellas.

Shortly after half past two, she was on her way home again, but had covered no more than about a third of the distance when the strap on her left sandal snapped. With nothing to anchor it to her foot, the sole flip-flopped uselessly around her ankle. And if that wasn't enough to cast a cloud on an otherwise perfect day, she then discovered that her cell phone battery had died and she couldn't call for help.

So, with at least another five kilometers still to go along a path never designed for barefoot travel, she had no choice but to struggle through the underbrush until she reached the highway. No easy task, certainly, but at least she then stood the chance of some kind soul stopping to offer her a lift.

A tour bus cruised past, followed by a stream of cars whose drivers were too intent on navigating the winding curves to spare a glance for a lone woman standing on the side of the road. After twenty minutes with no luck, she began plodding homeward, staying well on the shoulder to keep clear of the passing traffic, pausing hopefully every time she heard another vehicle approaching, only to find herself left in a blast of exhaust fumes and swirling dust.

Finally, when she'd given up waiting for a miracle that clearly wasn't going to happen, a pickup truck loaded with lumber came rattling around a bend. Realizing this, too, would probably pass her by if all she did was stick out a polite thumb, she took off her hat and waved it frantically to attract the driver's attention.

Catching sight of her, he braked and brought the vehicle to a stop a short distance farther along the road. Slapping on her hat, she clutched the framed print and hobbled to where the truck stood coughing out smelly fumes, and with the passenger door hanging open. By then, she was limping noticeably, crippled by the scorching heat from the pavement and the blister developing on the ball of her left foot.

"Thank you!" she panted, when she reached the open door. "You're a lifesaver!"

"Are you sure?" the driver inquired. "The last time we spoke, I got the distinct impression you thought I might be a murderer."

At the sound of that voice, her heart sank. In light of her insatiable fascination with him, running into her grandmother's neighbor was pretty much inevitable, but she'd have given her right arm for it not to happen with her again at a decided disadvantage.

Her hair was plastered to her scalp. Her blouse clung damply to her back, and she didn't want to know what her face looked like. Bad enough that it felt as if it could glow in the dark.

He lounged on the driver's side, one arm resting casually along the top of the steering wheel, the other hooked over the back of the vinyl-covered bench seat which was patched in places with duct tape. Once again, he wore faded blue jeans, and no shirt. Once again, he looked good enough to eat.

"What is it with you?" she snapped, averting her eyes from the sight of all that sleek muscle overlaid with smooth, sun-kissed skin. "Do you *always* have to go around showing off your body?"

"Only when I'm expecting company who'll be impressed by it," he replied, making no attempt at all to be discreet in his examination of her.

"Well, here's a news flash, Mr. Bertoluzzi. I'm not impressed."

Which was a bold-faced lie, of course.

His glance coasted the length of her. "I'm not impressed, either. I know crowned heads aren't generally renowned for their brainpower, but even the most dim-witted of royals know enough to wear decent walking shoes if they decide to travel on foot."

"My sandal broke."

"Sandals don't constitute walking shoes."

"I'm not the hiking boot type."

"What are you then, princess?"

"Not about to stand here all day, and listen to you lecturing me. Are you going to give me a ride, or not?"

"Why else do you think I stopped?"

"Then shut up and help me in," she flared, struggling to find a hold as she tried to haul her weary body up into the cab. He reached across, closed his hand around her wrist and gave a yank that brought her spilling in an ungainly heap across the bench, and left her lying facedown practically in his lap.

Dear God! The breath shot out of her in a winded whoof.

"A simple *grazie* will suffice," he remarked mildly. "And I'd appreciate it if you showed a little respect for my other passenger."

Struggling upright, she retrieved her hat from the floor and was about to ask *What other passenger?* when her glance fell on the bundle snuggled up next to him. No more than a couple of months old, a puppy, wrapped in his shirt, peeped out at her. Only by the grace of God had she avoided landing on top of it.

"Ohh!" she breathed, scooping up the little thing and cuddling it under her chin. "How adorable are you!"

But unlike the puppies she'd known, all of which would have responded to her overtures with wriggling, roly-poly ecstasy, this pathetic little bundle of bones managed only a feeble squirm. Even through the layers of shirt, she could feel the poor creature's ribs and what she could see of its black fur was dull and matted with dirt.

Peeling back a section of shirt, she examined the little thing more closely, then turned an accusing glare on her rescuer. "Is this your dog?"

"Who else's?"

"Then you should be ashamed!"

"Why's that, princess?"

That he should even have to ask! "He's thin as a rail, has fleas, probably worms as well, and a more sadly neglected puppy I've never seen. He needs veterinary attention. How long have you had him?"

"A couple of hours." He cut a quick glance her way, and added calmly, "And if it matters at all, he just piddled on your blouse."

"A couple of *hours?*" Taken aback, she chose to ignore his other gleeful item of information. "Well, why didn't you say so?"

"You didn't ask."

Exasperated, she rolled her eyes. "Okay, if that's the way you want to play it, answer me this: Where did you get him?"

He scowled. "Found him in a cardboard box in a back alley in Naples."

"You mean, you rescued him?"

"Yeah." He let out a long-suffering sigh. "Must be my day for picking up strays."

"Very funny, I'm sure." She nuzzled the puppy and stroked the tip of her finger down his head. "Was he the only one—in the box, I mean?"

He shot a withering look her way. "Isn't one enough?"

"I guess so." She hesitated a moment, then went on, "I've noticed you speak excellent English with a slight American accent."

"Is that a fact." He turned his attention back to the road.

"You're not very forthcoming, are you?"

A wry little smile tugged at his mouth. "Princess, I don't have to be. You've already heard from your rich grandmama everything there is to know about me."

"Not everything," she said, and dropped a kiss on the dog's little black nose. "She doesn't know you're a pushover for abandoned puppies."

He angled a glance at her. "She doesn't know you're riding in my truck, either. Imagine how she'll react when she finds out. Or is this to remain a secret between just the two of us?"

"Certainly not. I'm an adult. I don't have to run everything I do by my grandmother."

His glance veered to the left, and he gave a disbelieving snort under his breath. "If you say so, princess."

"I do. And I wish you wouldn't call me that. My name's Natalie."

"Hmm." He slouched lower on the bench and stared through the windshield.

Burying another surge of exasperation, she said, "And you're Damiano, right?"

"Wrong."

She ground down hard on her molars. "Then what?"

"You mean, Grandmama hasn't told you?"

"I wouldn't be asking, if she had. I know you're a Bertoluzzi, but that's about it."

"In these parts, that's more than enough." He swung off the busy corniche highway and followed the long private road leading to the waterfront estates fronting that section of the coast.

"Where do you want to be dropped off?"

"At my grandmother's gates. Where else?"

He shrugged. "Could be you don't want anyone to see you fraternizing with the enemy."

"I don't consider you my enemy, Mr. Bertoluzzi. As far as I'm concerned, you're simply the man next door—and you have one enormous chip on your shoulder."

He almost smiled. "And you're one nosy, opinionated woman."

"Who's very grateful that you happened to come along today when you did. I'd never have made it all the way home on foot."

"Just as a matter of interest, how come you were walking in the first place, instead of driving?"

"I just spent a week visiting an old friend in Rome, and we ate out a few times too often at too many fine restaurants. Not exactly the best way to stay in shape."

The leisurely way his glance roamed over her again made her wish she'd kept her mouth shut. "You're hardly ready to be roasted in the oven," he said, slowing marginally as he steered around a hairpin bend in the road.

"Thanks—I think! Any other little bits of wisdom you'd like to impart?"

"Yeah. The next time you feel disposed to burn off a few kilos, do yourself a favor first and invest some of that inherited wealth in a decent pair of shoes."

She stared at him sharply. "What do you know about my inheritance?"

"Figure it out for yourself," he replied, with yet another of his stock-in-trade small, knowing smiles. "Word gets out. Everybody in the area knows you're Signora Wade's only grandchild, and that she throws around enough money in one day to keep half the population of Naples in pasta and tomatoes for a year."

"I somehow don't think you're the kind of man who listens to idle gossip."

"You shouldn't be thinking about me at all," he informed her, pulling up before Villa Rosamunda's ornate iron gates. "Your grandmama's not the only one who wishes I'd drop off the face of the earth. Ask anyone, and they'll tell you I'm bad news. You're out of your league tangling with a man like me."

Ignoring the way her pulse leaped, she said, "I'm not scared of you."

"You should be," he said flatly.

"Thanks for the warning, but if you really want to live up to your lousy reputation, you'd better stop rescuing abandoned dogs. It doesn't fit the image you're working so hard to project." She gave the puppy one last kiss, deposited him gently next to his new owner, and was in the process of climbing down to the road when she stubbed her bare toe on the edge of a long, narrow cardboard box poking out from under the seat. "Ow!" she yelped. "What's in there?"

"A rifle," he drawled, with grim humor. "To keep trespassers like you off my property. Better watch your step in future."

"I don't believe you!"

He actually laughed then. "Your mistake, princess."

"I don't think so. I consider myself a pretty good judge of character, and you're not nearly the menace to society you make yourself out to be." She hopped out of the truck, plunked her hat back on her head and tucked the framed print under her arm. "Thank you again for the ride, Mr. Bertoluzzi."

"Uh-huh." Then, just as she was about to slam the door closed, he added, "The name's Demetrio, by the way."

A big, ridiculous smile spread across her face, as if he'd suddenly handed her half of Italy wrapped up in silk paper and tied with a broad satin ribbon.

"Demetrio?" A strong, proud name for a strong, proud man. "It suits you."

But she was left talking to herself. Gunning the engine, he continued down the road to where the gates to his property hung on rusted hinges.

He didn't wait to see her safely inside the house. He'd wasted enough time on her, and had more pressing matters needing his attention. A leaking roof to fix—and soon, if he wanted to preserve the painted ceiling in the master bedroom. Tiles to be laid, plumbing to upgrade, electrical wiring to be replaced...the list was endless. And now add caring for a pup to the list. *Dio*, he needed his head read!

Leaving the truck parked outside the garage which also served as his workshop, he carried the dog into the shade outside the kitchen door and put down a bowl of water, then found a packing crate to serve as a temporary kennel until he could fence off a portion of garden. He hadn't rescued the mutt from certain death in Naples, just to have it escape from his property and run under the wheels of a passing chauffeur-driven car in this tony neck of the woods.

With the dog safe, he turned back to the truck and tackled unloading supplies, beginning with the box under the cab seat. *Not a rifle, princess, but shelving for the pantry off the kitchen.*

Thinking of her made him smile. A strange sensation, that, and not one he was too familiar with of late, yet when he was around her, he couldn't seem to keep a straight face. And it was better to focus on why she amused him, than to dwell on his other responses to her.

She probably thought him an oaf, that he'd just sat and watched, instead of offering to help her down from the truck. Probably considered him socially impaired, too, the way he kept conversation to a bare minimum. But the truth wasn't quite that straightforward. Fact was, he'd known a lot of women in his time, but she was like none of them, and he didn't quite know how to deal with her. It was best, he decided, to stick to giving away nothing and maintaining his act, even though every part of him rebelled at the imposition.

He'd have had to be blind not to appreciate her coltish grace, the fine-boned delicacy of her wrists and fingers, the slender curve of her calf and well-turned ankles. Dead, not to want to touch her skin, so exquisitely fine and fair that just imagining how it would feel beneath his fingers left him short of breath and sent the blood pooling south of his waist. As for the thick, shining fall of her hair, he could almost see his reflection in it!

Furious with himself, he started on the pile of lumber stacked in the truck bed. It was late afternoon by then, and the sun enough to kill a man, but he didn't care. Driving himself to the point of physical exhaustion was his only guarantee that she'd fade from his mind. Yet despite his efforts, her face stubbornly remained front and center in his thoughts.

She was a thoroughbred through and through, no doubt about it, but it was more than just her looks and refinement that made her unforgettable. It was the way she'd responded to the dog. She cuddled and crooned to the scruffy little mutt as if it had a pedigree as long as his arm, and hadn't given a damn that it was making one devil of a mess on her expensive clothing.

Was he the only one? she'd asked, when he'd mentioned how he'd found the pup, and he'd more or less lied in his reply, because it would have hurt her too much to know he'd found three others, all dead.

Hell, it had hurt *him!* The difference was, he'd long ago learned to deal with whatever fate dished out. He doubted the same could be said of her.

The simple truth? She was little more than a puppy herself. Best of breed, perhaps, but about as naive and helpless as the mutt. And he couldn't afford to take on two like that. Best to shove her out of his mind and out of his life, and never let her back in again.

Easier said than done, though. Long after sunset, with the dog snoozing at his feet and a cold beer in his hand, he was still thinking about her, and wishing things were different.

Damn fool! As if anything could change who he was.

CHAPTER FOUR

THE name's Demetrio.

With just those three words, he put paid to any idea Natalie had of ignoring him. Not that she'd entertained much hope it would be possible anyway. Men like him—mysterious, slightly dangerous, and a whole lot alluring—weren't easily dismissed. Questions about him filled her mind like mushrooms popping up overnight in a fertile field. Throw a helpless puppy into the mix, and how could she not be completely hooked?

What made him tick? she wondered, waking the next morning to the sound of hammering from next door drifting through her open bedroom doors. He didn't appear to hold down a job, probably because no one would hire him. So how could he afford to restore a villa in such disreputable shape, especially one so large?

His truck, though serviceable enough, was old. Yet the back had been filled with expensive building materials. His fluency in English suggested either he was well traveled, well educated, and quite possibly both. Yet his hard, toned body pointed to a life of tough physical labor.

Maybe he came by all that in prison—worked on a chain gang by day, studied English by night...

Oh, please! She gave herself a mental shake. She was no better than anyone else, assuming the worst of him.

"You're looking very preoccupied, darling," her grandmother observed at breakfast.

"Yes." Natalie reflected a moment, then decided there was nothing to be gained by hiding secrets. "Something happened yesterday."

"I know. The Bertoluzzi man drove you home from town." Barbara looked pained. "In his truck."

"How did you know?"

"You were seen by a number of people, and are, consequently, the talk of the entire neighborhood."

"Which doesn't please you."

"Naturally not. Quite apart from the unsuitability of such an association, you're too young to be spending time alone with a man like him."

"I'm twenty-five, for heaven's sake! Old enough that my mother was knee-deep in wedding plans on my behalf, even though neither Lewis nor I was the least bit interested in getting married."

"Nevertheless, you're a babe-in-arms where that Bertoluzzi creature's concerned. Age has to do with a great deal more than years, Natalie. It has to do experience. His doesn't bear close inspection, and by comparison, yours is nonexistent."

"Then it's time I rectified that."

"With *him?*"

"Maybe." She met her grandmother's glance unflinchingly. "You don't have to approve of the people I associate with, Grandmother, but I demand you respect my right to choose them without first running their names by you."

"Well!" Barbara's face mirrored reluctant admiration. "You remind me of myself, when I was in my twenties. Hell-bent on going my own way, no matter how many obstacles were thrown in my path."

Affection for the one woman who'd always been her champion made Natalie smile. "I knew you'd see things my way."

"Up to a point only. Don't expect me to invite the man to dinner anytime soon. And for heaven's sake, use some common sense. Treating him with a modicum of civility is one thing—losing your heart to him quite another."

Hoping her flush went unnoticed, Natalie said, "That's a bit of a leap, don't you think? I'm talking about being neighborly, not indulging in an affair."

"Dear God, I should hope not! But I'm not so blind that I can't admit the rogue has a certain rugged charm. I can see how a young thing like you might find him quite appealing."

"Actually, it's his dog I'm in love with."

"I didn't know he had one."

Natalie laughed. "So some things *do* slip under your radar, after all?"

"It would appear so. What kind of dog?"

"It's a puppy still, and so pathetically undernourished that it's hard to tell what kind. I thought I'd raid the kitchen later on, and take over a bowl of scraps for the poor little thing. I'm not at all sure Demetrio can afford to feed him properly."

She realized her mistake the second his name popped out of her mouth. And her grandmother, of course, leaped on it with the alacrity of a terrier on a rat. "Oh, so it's *Demetrio* now, is it?" she inquired tartly. "Whatever happened to *Mr. Bertoluzzi*—or, better yet, *that man next door?*"

"No need to go into cardiac arrest, Grandmother. It's his name, that's all, and there's nothing unusual in that. Most people do have one, you know."

The snort of indignation provoked by *that* remark indicated she'd pushed the limits of her grandmother's tolerance far enough. "Think I'll take a dip in the pool. I'm finding it quite warm in here," she muttered, rising from the table, and fled the scene with rather more haste than grace.

When she followed the rutted path around the back of his house, just after one that same afternoon, she found him sitting with his back against a sunny wall, sharing cheese and bits of bread with the puppy.

"I thought you might want to give him these," she began, lifting the cover from a plastic container to show the meat and vegetable scrapings it contained.

Ignoring both the container and her suggestion, he eyed her from beneath the fringe of his dense black lashes, his glance taking her in from head to foot, and drawled, "You have a death wish, or something, woman?"

Just briefly, a quiver of fear shot over her. "What are you saying, exactly?"

"That if you persist in hanging around me, my bad reputation will rub off on you, and you won't be welcome at the posh soirees to which your grandmama's always invited."

Soirees, he said, and *to which your grandmama's invited,* he said, when he could just as well have made do with, *You won't get asked to the parties your old lady goes to.* Such sophisticated vocabulary and grammatically correct wording hardly fit the image of a thug with sinister deeds in mind.

Feeling foolish, she tried to relax and, not waiting to be invited, she sat down next to him, not quite close enough for any actual body contact, but close enough to be drawn helplessly into his aura. For a brief, insane moment, she knew a shocking urge to bury her face against his shoulder and drown in the warmth and scent of him.

For distraction, and because he scrambled around her feet

begging for attention, she hauled the puppy onto her lap and brought up a subject she'd already mentioned before. "Whoever taught you to speak English, Demetrio, did an outstanding job."

"Uh-huh." He looked away, his eyes glinting with amusement.

"You find that entertaining?"

"I find *you* entertaining, princess."

"And I find you interesting." She nuzzled the dog, puppy breath and all. "You probably don't want to hear this, but I like you, too."

"You talking to the dog?"

"No," she said. "I'm talking to you."

He swung his glance back to meet hers, all sign of amusement vanished. "You have no business liking me, and no business wandering over here whenever the mood takes you."

"Why not?"

His breath hissed in exasperation. "Because you don't have a clue what you're getting yourself into."

"My grandmother pretty much told me the same thing this morning. But I'm here anyway."

"You should listen to Grandmama. For once, she knows what she's talking about. A girl like you, able to take her pick from the best…" He gestured dismissively. "You ought to know better than to set your sights on a man like me."

"Well, first, I'm no girl. Second, I came to bring food for your dog because it's a neighborly thing to do, not because I wanted an excuse to size you up as possible husband material. And third, it turned out that the family my parents expected me to marry into decided *I* wasn't quite good enough for *them.* So don't bother spouting a lot of nonsense about us coming from different worlds, because I'm not buying it."

"The pedigreed boy-next-door didn't want to marry you?"

He shook his head, another flash of quiet laughter silvering his eyes. "Why not? Didn't his lobotomy work?"

She couldn't help herself. Latching on to the back-handed compliment, she said, "Does that mean *you* like me, Demetrio?"

His light blue gaze snapped to her face, the intensity in its depths such that goose bumps shivered the length of her spine. "It means like should stick to like, princess," he informed her flatly.

"That's a pretty old-fashioned attitude in this day and age, don't you think?"

"Really? You could have fooled me!" His laugh drew her gaze to his mouth, and she swallowed. She was no expert in the matter, but she'd have bet half her company shares that he could use that mouth in a way that would leave a woman sobbing with mindless pleasure.

Controlling her runaway thoughts, she said, "Just because some people around here don't want to know you doesn't mean everyone feels that way. I'm not in the habit of condemning a man because of the labels others pin on him. I prefer to judge him on the basis of personal experience." She nuzzled the puppy. "And I know you're a softie underneath that tough exterior. This little guy's proof of that."

"Dress it up in whatever fancy packaging you choose, but nothing changes the fact that I'm the last in a long line of Italian mobsters, and you're an American blue blood." He propped his elbows on his bent knees and squinted at the sky. "It comes down to the old saying about oil and water, princess. Stir them up all you like, they'll never mix."

Something—a nail, perhaps, or a rough piece of lumber—had gouged a wicked scratch down his forearm, and left blood to dry dark red against the deep bronze of his skin. Heedless of the consequences, she ran her finger lightly over the wound. "Speaking of water, have you washed and disinfected this?"

The muscle beneath his skin tensed. It was the only thing about him that moved. For the rest, he could have been hewn from granite.

A screaming silence charged the atmosphere, punctuated only by the soundless thud of her heart. Even the puppy grew quiet and settled sleepily in her lap.

She knew she should stop touching him, but her finger seemed welded to Demetrio's arm by a magnetic force far beyond her ability to withstand. Electrified, she stared. At his hands which, despite the nicks and calluses, were long-fingered and quite beautiful. At his strong, yet surprisingly elegant wrists.

The moment passed. Cursing, he manacled *her* wrist in a punishing grip. She inhaled sharply, her entire body coming alive. As if, with just one touch—and not a friendly one at that—he'd kindled a raging awareness within her that would eventually annihilate her.

He felt it, too, she could tell. He turned his face to hers and pinned her with a smoldering gaze. "You really do like playing with fire, don't you?" he rasped, his mouth inching toward hers. "How badly are you going to get burned, before you learn your lesson?"

She could feel the warm draft of his breath against her mouth. Knew in advance how his lips would taste. A painful, grinding hunger consumed her, one she'd have sold her soul to satisfy. "I don't know," she whispered recklessly. "Why don't you teach me?"

For a moment, she thought he might; that he'd kiss her and wrap his arms around her, and she'd sink under him, on the dry, dusty ground, and he'd pin her beneath his hard, powerful body, and all that strange, unsettling yearning coiling in her belly would tighten beyond bearing until…until…

Dashing her erotic fantasy to smithereens, he shoved her

away and leaped to his feet. "I'll tell you why. Because I've got plans for the rest of my life that don't include you."

If she possessed a fraction of that famous Wade pride so dominant in her grandmother, she'd have picked herself up off the ground, tossed him a glance designed to render him impotent, marched away without another demeaning word and permanently consigned Demetrio Bertoluzzi to hell.

She must not have suffered humiliation enough, though, because instead, she gestured to the container of food and protested, "But what about this? You surely aren't going to let it go to waste?"

As if what she'd brought was a priceless artifact, rather than table scraps. As if she was in the habit of losing sleep over leftovers. As if she'd go to any lengths, tolerate any amount of indignity, rather than sever her fragile link with a man who clearly valued his self-respect a lot more than she valued hers.

For pity's sake, what was the matter with her?

He rolled his eyes, tossed the dregs of his coffee into the hard-packed dirt and jerked his head toward the ramshackle kitchen. "If it means that much to you, drop the damned thing off in there on your way out. The mutt can have it later."

Then, before she had a chance to reply, he disappeared around the far side of the villa, his denim-clad legs eating up the distance in long, loping strides. He'd probably have denied it, but judging by the speed of his departure, she liked to imagine he was running away from her. A minute later, the screech of some sort of electric saw filled the air, putting an end to *that* absurd piece of wishful thinking.

Picking up his mug, she took it with the food scraps to the kitchen, the puppy gamboling at her heels. The remains of Demetrio's lunch were spread out on the makeshift table: a block of cheese, several slices of smoked meat, half a loaf of bread, a jar of ripe olives. An enamel coffeepot stood on the two-burner stove.

Surveying it all, Natalie shook her head. The food should be refrigerated and the dirty dishes removed, since both were a magnet for the flies buzzing at the window. Deciding it would take but a minute to restore the place to some sort of order, she set to work.

"Not that he'll thank me," she confided to the puppy, who was busy attacking her feet with every step she took, "but a man deserves better than to come home to a mess, after sweating in the broiling sun all afternoon."

The puppy wagged his stumpy tail in agreement, trotted over to his water bowl, stepped in it, lapped messily, then squatted under the table and left a puddle behind. Which, of course, she felt compelled to mop up. In fact, she decided, the entire floor would benefit from being swept. Dust and dirt had been tracked in from the garden, and collected in drifts around the holes left by broken floor tiles. Obviously housekeeping wasn't high on Demetrio's list of priorities.

Some might call her actions nothing but delaying tactics; others, unwarranted interference. She preferred to think of them as her good deed for the day and, humming under her breath, went in search of a broom, all the while accompanied by the puppy who continued to entertain himself by charging at her feet in a series of clumsy leaps. Fortunately the drone of power tools continued outside, drowning out her laughter and his excited yips.

She hadn't actually intended to trespass beyond the kitchen, but when the dog disappeared through the door leading to the rest of the house, what choice did she have but to follow? She'd noticed that Demetrio had built a kind of holding pen in the corner of the kitchen, a clear indication that he didn't want his rescued pet having the run of the place.

Chasing the little imp down a wide passageway, she ended up in a grand hall adjacent to a small entrance foyer where the front door was located. Paved in black and white marble squares, it resembled a giant chessboard and was large enough to serve as a ballroom for a hundred guests or more. A grimy but gorgeous chandelier hung by a length of chain from its high, domed ceiling. A branched staircase, rising to the right of where she stood, led to a landing which ran around three sides of the upper floor, and ended in a minstrel's gallery over the front door.

To her left, an archway opened into what was probably a huge, formal dining room, with built-in china cabinets filling one wall. Next to it was a library lined with glass-fronted bookshelves.

A long, elegantly proportioned salon running the entire depth of the house lay opposite the staircase. All three areas boasted marble fireplaces and beveled glass doors accessing a covered terrace. With the puppy in tow, Natalie wandered from one room to the next, both enthralled and saddened by the sights confronting her.

Ceilings adorned with faded frescoes soared some twelve feet above inlaid wooden floors. Marble pillars flanked the open archways. Intricate moldings surrounded the doors to the terrace. Deep, carved baseboards ran around the perimeter of the floors. And all of it scarred by damage willfully inflicted.

Holes had been punched in the plaster walls, tiles smashed in the hearths, and floorboards pulled up in places, their jagged ends protruding like broken limbs. If these three rooms reflected the general state of the villa, how painful it must have been for Demetrio to come home again.

How could he ever hope to restore it all? Yet the signs of his work were everywhere: scaffolding erected in the salon;

hand-painted tiles arranged neatly beside the fireplaces; cans of paint stacked in the corners.

Rescuing the puppy before he devoured a wad of moth-eaten chair stuffing he'd come across, she picked him up and approached the one item left untouched by malicious mischief. Leaning against the wall beside the fireplace in the salon was a large black and white wedding photograph in a dusty gold frame.

She guessed, from the clothes the couple wore, that it must have been taken in the mid-1950s. The bride was a pretty young thing, perhaps only about twenty years old, with dark hair, dark haunted eyes—a strange manifestation in a bride, Natalie thought—and a mouth that seemed oddly familiar.

Demetrio's mouth, she realized, kneeling for a closer inspection.

But the groom…? She shuddered. Even in a photograph faded from exposure to time and too much sun, he gave her the creeps. He looked into the lens of the camera with the glacial stare of a man completely devoid of human warmth: strikingly tall, unquestionably handsome—and totally deadly.

She was so shaken that she didn't realize she was no longer alone until a shadow fell across the floor. Expecting a verbal onslaught for again snooping where she didn't belong, she sprang to her feet, so full of startled guilt that she let the puppy slip from her lap. But the man who'd entered the room via the double doors to the terrace and was now closing in on her was not Demetrio.

No more than five feet eight or nine, with iron-gray hair and a neatly trimmed mustache, he looked to be in his late sixties. He wore a cream linen suit, and carried a Panama hat. Sunlight winked on the diamond of his tie pin and bounced off the dark reflective lenses of his glasses.

He smiled, revealing a gold tooth—a parody of a gangster,

belonging more to Hollywood than the Amalfi coast, she thought, stifling a burst of laughter that hinged dangerously close to hysterical, because there was nothing remotely amusing about the evil miasma emanating from this individual.

"Buona sera," he said.

His whispery greeting made her blood run cold. Instinctively she reached for the puppy but, with the fearless curiosity natural to a young animal, he eluded her and trotted forward to investigate the intruder.

Beating her to it, the man bent, grabbed the dog by the scruff of its neck and hoisted it high. The poor little thing whimpered in protest, its paws flailing in midair.

Natalie gasped, almost suffocating with a fear so real that it seemed to darken the air around her. "Give him to me!"

"But of course, *signorina.*" Threat implicit in his softly uttered response, in his smile, in his every gesture, the man extended his arm and dangled the pup high in the air.

She knew without a shadow of a doubt that the little creature's life hung by a thread. That this intruder, whose smile could not for a moment hide the cruel twist of his mouth, would think nothing of letting go and allowing the poor thing to smash in a heap of broken bones on the floor at her feet.

"Oh, please!" she begged, jumping up in a futile attempt to rescue the hapless puppy. *"Please* don't hurt him."

The man swung the little body back and forth like a pendulum. "Why not?" he whispered.

With the last of the two-by-sixes cut to size, Demetrio laid down the saw, figuring he'd take a break and maybe swim a few laps in the pool. Only when he turned his head aside to swipe the back of his hand over his brow did he notice the car drawn up under the portico at the front of the villa. Long, black and sleek, with smoke-tinted windows, it bore a chilling resemblance to the kind of vehicle he'd too often seen drive up to the villa when he'd lived there as a boy.

Approaching the house from the front, he heard voices wafting through the open windows of the salon, one soft and male and lethal, the other feminine and breathy with terror.

The realization that Natalie was not long gone from the scene, as he'd assumed, almost brought Demetrio to his knees. Suddenly he was running, taking the front steps three at a time, his mouth filled with the coppery taste of fear.

If she'd been hurt because of him, he'd kill the man responsible.

He pushed the thought aside, unable to confront the possibility. She was persistent, intrusive and annoying as hell. But she was also young, beautiful and rich, and that made her the perfect hostage. For him to go roaring in there, full of reckless fury, would put her in even greater danger than that which she already faced. The heroics would have to wait for another time. Cold, measured focus was what he needed now.

Moving stealthily along the terrace, he made his way to the seaward side of the house and inched toward the salon's French doors, angling himself against the outer wall in such a way that he could see inside the room without being noticed by its occupants.

There were just the two of them: Natalie, and a man he didn't recognize. Neither had heard his approach. They were too engrossed in each other—the visitor radiating a menace so real, it was almost tangible, and Natalie trying to contain her terror—to have the slightest awareness that a third member had joined the party.

Hammer swinging in one hand, Demetrio stepped quietly into the room, closed in on the man standing with his back to him, and tapped him on the shoulder. "Looking for me, *signor?*" he inquired coldly.

CHAPTER FIVE

SILENCE greeted his question, spinning out like some toxic spiderweb and humming with unspoken threats on both sides. Then turning his head just enough to reveal his profile, the man said, "I am indeed, Signor Bertoluzzi, but happened across your beautiful wife instead."

Something vaguely familiar about him left an unpleasant taste in Demetrio's mouth. Pinning the visitor in an unblinking stare, he said, "The lady is not my wife, she is my guest. Kindly let her have her dog, then we'll discuss what business you think you have with me."

The man smiled. Not a pretty sight. "Of course," he murmured, continuing to dangle the pup just out of her reach. "Here, *signorina*. He's all yours."

Natalie stepped toward him uncertainly, and when she hesitated, clearly not trusting him to keep his word, he gave the pup a vicious shake. "Take him," he taunted, his voice a whisper of evil threading the atmosphere.

"Do as he says, Natalie," Demetrio said evenly, never once taking his eyes off the man.

Scraping up her courage, she rushed forward and, by the grace of a benign God, managed to catch the pup just as the visitor let it fall from his hands. Rage fueling a rush of adrenaline that had his heart thundering against his ribs, Demetrio spoke to her again. "Please leave us now, and take the dog with you."

She obeyed, clutching the pup to her breast. She was trembling so hard, he didn't know how she managed to hang on to the dog, let alone put one foot in front of the other and scuttle from the room.

He watched until she was out of sight and earshot before turning his attention again to his visitor. "You know my name, *signor*, but I have no idea of yours."

"Cattanasca," the man replied. "Guido Cattanasca."

Ignoring his outstretched hand, Demetrio said flatly, "I have no idea why you're in my house, Signor Cattanasca, but I suggest you make the most of the opportunity because, not for any reason at all, are you welcome ever to come back again."

Cattanasca smiled and shrugged. "You might change your mind, when I explain."

"I sincerely doubt it."

"Yes?" Cattanasca smiled again, a thin, unpleasant twisting of his lips beneath his perfectly trimmed gray mustache. "You don't recognize me, do you, Demetrio?"

"Should I?"

"Well, we have met before, although you were just a boy at the time. I occasionally visited your grandfather. He and I were quite good friends and spent many a pleasant hour sitting in the shade of that veranda out there, enjoying a glass of wine together."

"If you were a friend of my grandfather's, you're doubly unwelcome here. I don't share his taste in *friends*."

"Oh, no need to look so affronted, young man! I'm quite harmless which, I admit, is more than could be said of Ovidio at times. For many years now, I've been involved in the local real estate market, mostly as a developer, and am, in fact, the man who made it possible for your grandfather to buy this house, something for which he was always grateful."

Demetrio doubted his grandfather had ever been grateful to a living soul for anything. "And you're here now because?"

"I came to make you an offer," Cattanasca said, nonchalantly admiring his manicure. "I'm willing to buy this property, and give you a very good price for it."

"Then you wasted your time. It's not for sale."

Cattanasca laughed softly. "My dear boy, sooner or later everything's for sale. It's simply a matter of arriving at the price the prospective buyer's willing to pay."

"Perhaps in your circles, but not in mine."

"Stubborn, just like your grandfather," Cattanasca murmured, sparing his fingernails one last glance. "But not, it would seem, one-tenth as smart."

The comparison to his grandfather, favorable or otherwise, sparked a fresh outburst of fury in Demetrio, and ratcheted up his adrenaline to an even more dangerous level. "I suggest you leave now, before this discussion becomes irritating." He swung the hammer menacingly, just to be sure his point came across. "In case I haven't already made it clear, you're not welcome here, Signor Cattanasca. Not today, not tomorrow, not ever."

"No need to threaten me with violence, Demetrio," Cattanasca replied soothingly, although he had the good sense to take a precautionary step backward. "Contrary to what you seem to believe, that's not how business is done, these days. But before you dismiss me as being beneath your notice, take a look around and tell me: how do you expect to resurrect this place single-handedly?"

Struggling to keep his rage in check, Demetrio jerked his chin at the holes punched in the plaster walls, the ripped up floorboards. "A more relevant question is, how do you suppose it came to be in such sad shape to begin with?"

"It's a shame what can happen when a house is left empty for too long." His visitor's smile oozed ersatz sympathy. "*Ragazzini* of today…who knows what they're capable of?"

"*Ragazzini?*" Demetrio kicked one of the tiles which had been ripped away from the fireplace surround. "Kids who vandalize for entertainment don't do this kind of damage. They break windows, smash dishes, steal booze. You and I both know this isn't kids' doing. This is systematic destruction with a fixed purpose in mind."

Stepping closer, he matched Cattanasca's smile, his own tight and feral. "You want to know what I think? That someone looking to take advantage of the vandals' handiwork is responsible—but you wouldn't know anything about that, would you, Cattanasca?"

"Certainly not!" Cattanasca dusted off his lapels, as if the mere idea left him feeling unclean. "I'm a legitimate businessman making you a legitimate offer."

"Which I have refused."

"So it would seem. But face it, my young friend. You're hemorrhaging money on this place, and if you continue to do so, you're going to bleed to death. So again, I urge you—be smart. Give my offer second thought."

"Not in this lifetime. Now get the hell off my property before I break your nose."

"Dear me, I think your grandfather would be rather proud of you, after all! There's hope for you yet, my boy."

"But none for you, Cattanasca. There isn't enough money in the world that can convince me to let you get your hands on this house, or the land it sits on."

"That's your final word?"

"That's my final word."

"Then I wish you luck."

"I don't need luck."

"We all need luck, my hotheaded young friend. Accidents happen, and who knows how or where they might next strike?" He stroked his hand down a nearby marble pillar. "A beautiful piece, this. It would be a pity to see it destroyed, and all your hard work for nothing, should some unfortunate incident occur."

There was no "should" about it. Demetrio knew that, as surely as he knew his own name. He'd just been issued an ultimatum. The question was, what were his options in dealing with it?

He knew how his grandfather would have responded. Just like every Bertoluzzi before him. With violence. Cattanasca's body would have washed up somewhere along the shore with a bullet hole in his forehead. Demetrio could pick up where they'd left off, and fight as they'd have fought, or he could hold true to a promise he'd made fourteen years ago, and take a stand for justice and honor.

There was never any question but that his promise would rule the day. "Off my property, Cattanasca. *Now!*"

Cattanasca pursed his wrinkled lips and smoothed the brim of his expensive Panama. "No need to get your tail feathers in a ruffle, dear boy. I'll leave. But if I may offer a parting word of advice, I suggest you watch your blood pressure and adopt a more conciliatory attitude toward life in general. *Ciao!*"

"It's okay," Natalie murmured, sinking to the floor near the makeshift dog pen and cuddling the puppy. "You're safe now."

But who was she really trying to convince? Not the puppy, that was certain. He'd curled up in her arms and fallen asleep, blissfully ignorant of the fact that, yet again, his fragile little life had hung in the balance, or that, both times, he had Demetrio to thank for saving him.

"...*get the hell off my property before I break your nose.*"

"*Dear me, I think your grandfather would be rather proud of you, after all! There's hope for you yet, my boy.*"

"*But none for you, Cattanasca...*"

"It's cats who are supposed to have nine lives, not dogs," she went on desperately, because even the sound of her own babbling was better than the snatches of conversation drifting down the hall, the stranger's voice sibilant and chilling, and Demetrio's deep tones vibrating with rage. "You're too little and skinny to defend yourself, even if you do have the biggest feet I've ever seen. You need to smarten up, if you want to survive. You can't go running up to just anybody and assume they're your friends. There are a lot of bad people in this world, munchkin."

"You'd better start taking your own advice," Demetrio advised her tersely, striding into the kitchen. "You just ran afoul of a man I trust about as much as I would a starving boa constrictor."

Carefully, so as not to disturb him, she parked the dog on the blanket in his holding pen, and scrambled to her feet. "Why was he here?"

"More to the point, why are *you?* I told you to leave."

"I thought you just meant I should leave the other room."

"Then you thought wrong," he said flatly.

"I didn't want to leave the puppy alone. That man was cruel, Demetrio! You should have seen the way he handled your dog. I was afraid he was really going to hurt the poor little thing."

"Lucky for you, he didn't, although I wouldn't put it past him."

Nausea rose up in her. The people she knew didn't behave that way toward animals. They treated them as members of the family. "Is he a friend of yours?"

Demetrio's laughter rang out, bitter as unripe lemons. "I'm not that desperate! But he claims he was a friend of my grandfather's."

"He's...*evil*." A winterlike chill crept over her. Shivering, she hugged her elbows. "I could feel it coming off him like a cold November fog."

"Which makes for a good reason to stay away, right?"

"I'm not worried for myself. You're the one he's after." He didn't like having her invade his physical space. Had told her quite plainly to go away and leave him alone. But the man who'd visited him spelled danger as plainly as if he wore a sign around his neck proclaiming the fact.

Anxious to convey her concern, she edged closer and once more risked Demetrio's anger by laying her hand on his arm. "I wasn't able to hear everything the two of you talked about, but I understood enough to sense he poses some sort of threat." She shuddered with distaste. "It was there in his voice. I think you should notify the police."

Again, at the physical contact, tension ran through him. "And tell them what? That a woman who hardly knows me is worried that I can't look after myself?"

"Well, what if you can't? What if you're no match for a man like him?" Another shiver pinpricked her skin. "This might sound melodramatic to you, but I think he might be a crook."

Demetrio rolled his eyes dramatically. "Stop it, princess. You're scaring me."

"Make fun of me all you like, but I trust my instincts. A man who'd terrorize a puppy?" She shuddered. "There's no limit to what else he might do."

This time, Demetrio initiated contact, touching her cheek with his long, strong fingers. "Natalie, calm down," he said gently. "You're letting your imagination run away with you. The guy's unpleasant, but he's not a criminal and he's not going to come after me in the dead of night with a knife. He's a local businessman with a reputation to maintain, however shabby it might be."

"But why was he here?"

"He wants to buy my house."

"Are you going to sell it to him?"

"No."

"Will he bother you again, do you think?" The question trembled from her lips, and the fear she thought she'd conquered came back to haunt her with a vengeance.

"He might." The steel in his voice sent icy thrills up her spine. "Regardless, I'll be ready for him."

"And do what? Reason with him?" She curled her fingers around his wrist, urgency vibrating through her, and lifted her face to his, beseeching him with her eyes to take her seriously. "I don't want you to get into trouble over a man like him. I don't want anything bad to happen to you, Demetrio."

For a long, intense moment, he neither moved nor spoke. Then his hand covered hers and drew her closer. "Too late for that," he murmured, the look he turned on her smoldering with blue fire. "*You're* happening, princess, and that's about as bad as things can get."

Earlier, when they sat outside, she'd thought he was going to kiss her and had suffered a gnawing disappointment when he didn't. This time, she expected nothing—except, perhaps, another brush-off—and he caught her unprepared, with her mouth quite literally hanging open.

Before she had a chance to close it, he covered it with his and, all liquid, fiery hunger, laid siege to her. Forget rejection, distance, indifference. This was the kiss of a man driven by a passion as acute as it was sudden, and she melted under its heat. If she lived to be a hundred, she knew it would remain seared forever in her memory.

That she responded with matching fervor was something beyond her control. At that moment, all she knew, all she cared about, was the taste and feel and scent of him: the sun-kissed smell of his skin; the firm, smooth texture of his lips; his hand stroking up her neck to cup her jaw; his arm pulling her close against him; his tongue sweeping the dark enclave of her mouth and stealing its secrets.

And still it wasn't enough to satisfy the craving which had been building in her from the moment she first laid eyes on him. He was as alien to her world as if he'd flown in from another planet. Where other men she knew deemed conformity as crucial an accessory as their fraternity rings and expensive watches, he was an unabashed rebel. The citizens of this community considered him completely beyond redemption. A threat to decent, law-abiding society.

And if they were right? If the threat she'd heard him utter to Cattanasca was real?

At that moment, she didn't care. All she wanted was more of him.

Was this what a too-close brush with danger did to a man and a woman? she wondered, dazedly. Did it derive its being from the same primal need that motivated near-strangers on the brink of destruction, to mate and procreate?

Then, as the hunger ran amok inside her, she stopped trying to wrestle reason out of madness. What was the point, with her thoughts fragmented, her mind a rich, exotic tapestry of emotion, her body a crucible of sensation?

Behind her closed eyes, sunspots danced, ringed with whirling prisms of pure gold. Her knees turned rubbery and she started to tremble again, but from desire this time, not fear.

A rushing wind filled her ears. Her blood, she realized dimly, and, afraid she might faint, clutched a fistful of Demetrio's shirt to anchor herself upright.

He walked her backward, stopping only when the edge of the makeshift table pressed against her bottom. His hand slid down her side. Settled at her hip.

He molded her to him, nudged one knee between both of hers. The weathered fabric of his jeans scraped the tender inner skin of her thighs exposed by her shorts. The calluses on the thumb of his other hand rasped lightly down her throat.

It was more body contact than she'd ever thought to share with him, but it wasn't nearly enough. Her breasts ached for his touch, leaving her nipples beaded hard as pebbles. Tiny electrical impulses throbbed between her legs, and if his hand had strayed there, he'd have found her silky and swollen and shamelessly eager.

She'd remained a virgin from choice until that moment when, suddenly, fiercely, virginity became a burden she couldn't wait to shed. Never mind that the setting left much to be desired—a rough sheet of plywood, broken floor tiles underfoot, a cavernous kitchen on the brink of decay. If he'd pursued the matter, she'd have let him take her, and it would have been glorious.

Sadly—or perhaps wisely—he saved her from herself and him. Rearing back, he stared at her, his gaze unfocused. Then, as reality swam back to engulf him, he shoved her away. "What the devil!" he muttered, and wiped a savage hand over his mouth, as if to erase the taste of her.

Staggering to maintain her balance, she gripped the table top, all the lovely, erotic sensations he'd evoked chased away by the absolute contempt she saw in his eyes. The unfinished edge of the plywood dug into hand and embedded a row of tiny, painful slivers in the soft pads of her fingertips.

"Demetrio...?" she began, dismayed.

But he didn't allow her to finish. Grabbing her by the upper arm, he marched her out into the warm, golden afternoon and pointed her firmly in the direction of the path leading to the road. "Stop being such a damned fool, and stay the hell away from me and out of my business," he roared.

If he'd spoken with his usual exasperated restraint, she might have obeyed. Might have been convinced that he really did want rid of her. But his bellow of rage betrayed a depth of feeling that went far beyond annoyance. He was afraid—for her, and of her.

Elated that he couldn't drum up the indifference he tried so hard to project, she shook him off. "No," she said. "There's a connection between us, Demetrio. I felt it from the first, and so did you. And that makes what happens to you very much my business."

"You watch too many soap operas," he retorted scathingly.

"Even if that were true, it wouldn't change how I feel."

Jamming his hands in his hip pockets, he glared at the inoffensive sky. "If you're hoping to pass the time with a summer fling, princess, you'll have to look elsewhere. I've got work waiting."

"I know," she said. "And I'm going to help you get it done."

"Soil those lily-white hands? Break one of those perfectly polished nails?" He laughed out loud, all trace of mockery gone. "I'll believe that when I see it!"

"Then prepare to be converted." She spun away from him, grabbed a rake leaning against the wall, and furiously started gathering up odds and ends of lumber scattered near the house.

"Cut it out!" he snapped. "You can't do that."

"Who says?"

"I do. You're not designed for this kind of work."

He went to take away the rake, but she skipped out of reach. "You forget, I'm Barbara Wade's granddaughter."

On the second attempt, he caught her and grabbed the rake. "And that means...?"

"That she didn't get to where she is today, president of her own financial empire, by sitting back and letting others do the work for her. She marched right into the so-called man's world and got her hands every bit as dirty as yours, even if it was only metaphorically. And guess what, Demetrio? I'm no different."

"You might not think so, but—"

"I *know* so! I'm a fast learner, I'm stubborn, and I tackle what has to be done without shying away if it happens to be different from what I'm used to. Show me how to patch holes in plaster, and I'll do it. Show me how, and I'll polish windows, wash floors, paint walls."

He sighed and rolled his beautiful blue eyes despairingly. "You're not going to go away, are you?"

"No," she said, shaking her head for added emphasis. "So you might as well get used to the idea and give in gracefully."

"Fine." He shrugged and handed back the rake. "Knock yourself out. When you're done out here, there's a whole mess of stuff needing to be swept up inside, as you no doubt noticed on your self-conducted tour of the place."

CHAPTER SIX

SHE'D last about fifteen minutes at most, he figured. Which was a good fourteen minutes more than was safe for either one of them. By hanging around, she created a distraction he'd never been less able to afford. Worse, by being in the wrong place at the wrong time, she found herself at the mercy of the kind of man no decent woman should ever have to encounter.

Demetrio still broke out in a sweat at the thought of her alone in a room with Cattanasca, a man utterly without conscience who wouldn't hesitate to use anyone, or anything, to further his own ends. Exactly what that might entail might be open to question, but Demetrio had a pretty clear picture of the possibilities. Cattanasca operated on the right side of the law—by a hair's breadth only.

She'd realized it, too, albeit after the fact, as Demetrio realized when he discovered her huddled on the floor in the kitchen, next to the dog pen. The pallor of her skin, the distress darkening her eyes, and the fine trembling of her body painted a graphic picture.

Not that that excused his reaction. To kiss her, hold her, taste the wild sweetness of her...! He shook his head in self-disgust. He was dealing with enough complications, and didn't need to add sex with an American heiress to the mix.

Unaware of his gloomy introspection, Natalie wielded the rake with a vengeance, creating a cloud of dust as she amassed a respectable pile of debris. When she saw him watching her, she stopped, braced a fist on one hip, and glared at him in mock indignation.

"Hey, I offered to help, not take over the whole job so you can slack off!" she said, blowing a wisp of hair off her face. "How about you make yourself useful, and find something I can load this mess into?"

She was too lovely. Too appealing. And there was a lot more to her than wealth and fine lineage. She had grit and courage and spirit. She brought out the best in him. With a woman like her at his side, he could...

Son of a bitch! Choked with sudden emotion, he spun on his heel and disappeared into the four-car garage. The Ferrari occupied a quarter of the space, covered by a protective canvas, but the rest of the area he'd turned into a storage area for various tools and equipment, as well as a workshop. He found a wheelbarrow, loaded a shovel and a pair of heavy gloves in it, and hauled it back to where she'd resumed working.

"You'd better use these," he said brusquely, tossing the gloves to her.

"Thanks."

She dropped the rake and pulled them on. They were ludicrously oversized, swallowing up her dainty hands and forearms like some coarse giant mouth. She could have fit both feet in just one of them, if she'd tried, and still had room to spare.

The thought sent his glance skimming to her legs, and he forced himself to look away as sweat beaded his brow again, for reasons that had nothing to do with the punishing heat of the sun. There was only one cure for what ailed him: to immerse himself in work until he was too tired to *spell* sex, let alone think about engaging in it. That, and do whatever it took to discourage her from dropping by whenever the mood took her.

He could only hope that, as proverbs went, "out of sight, out of mind" came closer to the truth than "absence makes the heart grow fonder."

"See yourself off the premises, when you're done," he told her, knowing he sounded surly and wishing it could have been otherwise. Given a different history, he'd have pursued her, and let those who didn't like it stew in their own juice. But there was no escaping who he was. He might not have earned his lousy reputation, but he'd certainly inherited it, and putting the moves on Natalie was no way to better his image in that wealthy Italian enclave of high society.

"You're leaving?"

The disappointment in her question tore at him. *Not from choice, princess!* "I'm leaving. I've got phone calls to make."

"For more supplies?"

"Uh-huh." Specifically, hiring a local outfit to erect a fifteen-foot-high wall between the front of his property and the road, ordering custom-built remote-controlled iron gates to replace those currently in use, and installing a comprehensive alarm system. And until all these were in place, padlocking a sturdy chain around the old gates to keep them shut.

The next time Cattanasca decided to drop in for a visit, he wouldn't find it so easy to access the place.

And just as important, nor would she.

Two hours later, with the afternoon winding down, he had reason to question his last assumption. His work done for the day, he came through the house to the kitchen and looked out the back, expecting she'd be long gone. Instead he found her still hard at it. She'd finished piling the construction debris into the wheelbarrow and was on her knees, yanking weeds from what had once been his grandmother's herb garden.

Hardly the picture of a woman easily put to rout, even though exertion had taken its toll. She'd abandoned the work gloves, and was tackling the job with her bare hands. She'd found a sliver of lumber no wider than a chopstick and used it to skewer her glorious hair in a knot on top of her head, leaving her pale, fragile nape exposed.

She'd taken off her blouse and draped it over a nearby shrub. Underneath, she wore a skinny little tank top stained with a patch of sweat down the back. Her face was flushed a deep rose, and she was covered in dust.

Defeated, he took a couple of beer from the refrigerator, let the dog out of its pen and went out to join her. "Okay, that's enough," he groused. "There are laws against slave labor in this part of the world. Time to call it a day."

For once, she didn't argue. Easing painfully to her feet, she followed him into the shade and collapsed next to him in the long grass.

"Here." He snapped the tab on one of the beer cans and passed it to her.

"Thanks," she said, her voice thin with fatigue.

The dog crawled into her lap and nuzzled her bare thighs.

Demetrio blinked, looked away and took a long swig from his own can before he trusted himself to glance her way again. "You're welcome. You've earned a break."

"We both have." She took a sip of her beer and made a face.

Noticing, he said tersely, "Sorry it's not champagne, princess."

"I'm not complaining. I just don't care for the taste of beer, that's all." But she sipped again anyway, closed her eyes and cradled the frosty can to her cheek, then slid it languidly down her throat to the low-cut neck of her tank top.

This time, he didn't look away soon enough to prevent a bolt of desire shooting, hot and fierce, to the pit of his stomach. He envied that can. Wanted to sweep his tongue over the dew of condensation it left gleaming on her skin. Wanted to touch her all over and steal the very essence of her.

At such close quarters, her scent wrapped around him, a heady mixture of shampoo and woman and freshly turned earth. But if she'd been mucking out a stable and hadn't washed her hair in a week, his response would have been just the same. Everything about her—the way her breasts rose gently when she lifted her hand to anchor her unruly topknot, the absent grace with which she caressed the dog—left him dizzy with hunger and brought the memory of their kiss into sharp focus again.

Who was he fooling? He'd never forget the sweet innocence of her mouth, the trust with which she'd come into his arms. Never stop wanting more of the same.

Dio! In her own way, she spelled more trouble than Cattanasca.

"A penny for your thoughts," she remarked, turning her head and catching him off guard. "Or should I say a euro?"

She had a smear of dirt on her nose which begged to be wiped away, but he knew if he touched her that it wouldn't end there. "I was figuring out my next move," he replied, and given the trend of his thoughts, it wasn't a complete lie.

She cast a glance across the garden to the towering walls of the villa, and shook her head. "You've embarked on a mammoth undertaking with this place. Are you sure you'll be able to manage it?"

"I wouldn't have started the job if I didn't know I could finish it."

She tipped her head inquiringly. "Why is it so important to you, Demetrio? Wouldn't it be easier to start afresh somewhere else, with something smaller?"

"I don't do 'easy,' and even if I did, I'd never sell this place. It was my grandmother's home. She treasured everything you see inside these garden walls. It would break her heart to know the state it's all in now."

"Even so, the amount of labor involved is huge. And to take it on all by yourself? If you're determined to keep the place, wouldn't it make more sense to hire someone locally to put it back in shape?"

He laughed. "You really are naive, Natalie. Who do you think would work for me?"

"People who respect the fact that you're trying to preserve an architectural treasure and restore it to its former glory, perhaps."

"Winning other people's respect doesn't top my list of priorities. The main reason I'm doing this is that it matters to me, and because I can."

"But how can you afford—?" She stopped, and looked as if she'd bitten off the end of her tongue. "I guess I don't have the right to ask you that."

"No, you don't. It's none of your business what I can or can't afford."

A flash of indignation sparked in her lovely gray eyes. "Well, please rest assured I won't make the same mistake again! But even someone as naive as you think I am can see it has to be costing you plenty, and you're not even halfway finished yet, so forgive me for being concerned."

"Concerned, curious—call it what you like, the bottom line remains the same. It's my business, not yours."

A brittle silence followed. She let it run its course for a full minute or more before setting down her beer can and shooing the dog off her lap. "Then I'll leave you to enjoy it in solitude since I've clearly outstayed my welcome."

"Such as it was to begin with," he muttered, not nearly as

relieved by her imminent departure as common sense told him he should have been.

"Such as it was, indeed," she agreed loftily, climbing to her feet and reclaiming her blouse. "Thank you for your hospitality. I'll do us both a favor and not impose on you again."

"Good."

She made it all the way to the road before she started to cry. *Oh, honestly!* she thought, scrubbing furiously at the tears tracking down her face. The way she was carrying on, anyone would think she'd just been left at the altar when, in fact, she'd been handed the perfect excuse to part company with a man so closemouthed and standoffish that it was small wonder people couldn't warm to him.

She knew she'd been out of line to question his finances, but the way he'd rebuffed her, with such hostility, had set her to thinking things she wished she could ignore.

He bought his supplies in Naples, a city whose dark underbelly too often overshadowed its rich cultural heritage and many splendid attractions. Drug trafficking and gang warfare thrived in certain areas.

Was *that* how he could afford the renovation—by seeking out black-market goods through shady underworld connections? Or was it simply that he was too proud to risk being turned away by legitimate retailers in the immediate area who believed that the sins of the father were automatically visited upon the son?

She didn't have the answers. All she knew for certain was that she felt bereft and sad that something full of promise had been killed before it had a chance to bloom.

What was it about him that drew her so inexorably? That in him, she'd found her soul mate? Or was it his being forbidden fruit that enticed her so?

She'd never seen herself as the kind of woman who liked to flirt with danger, but the underlying thrill of it had shaped every hour since he'd blasted into her life. Was it being suddenly set free from it that made the world seem so silent and empty now?

"You look bedraggled, my darling," her grandmother observed, when she let herself into the house. "Not your usual pristine self at all. Why don't you take a long, refreshing bath, then put on something pretty and come with me to the Sorrentinos' for cocktails and dinner? Marianna phoned half an hour ago to invite us. Her nephew, Augusto, is visiting from Venice. You might enjoy meeting him."

Natalie couldn't imagine a worse fate than spending the evening pretending to find another man fascinating. "Thanks, but not tonight. I have the beginnings of the most ferocious headache and plan to turn in early."

It wasn't quite a lie, but it would be, if she accepted the invitation.

"Hmm." Her grandmother frowned. "You do seem a little peaked. Quite red-eyed, in fact."

"Too much sun, probably," she said quickly, no more able to withstand Barbara's close inspection than she was to feign interest in a man who probably didn't want to be saddled with her company any more than she did with his. "I went out without a hat again. You'd think I'd know better by now. Go ahead without me, Grandmother, and I'll see you in the morning."

She took a long, relaxing bath, and had just climbed out of the tub and into a cool cotton robe, and was about to order a light snack in her room, when one of the housemaids tapped on her door.

"You're wanted on the phone, Signorina Cavanaugh. A gentleman caller."

Her father, she supposed, flopping onto the bed and lifting the receiver. She couldn't imagine who else it might be.

But the voice flowing down the line and drizzling over her like sun-kissed honey possessed nothing of her father's Maryland intonation. "What are you doing at this very minute, princess?"

No, *Hello, how are you?* No, *Hope I'm not disturbing you.* No, *Sorry I was such a jerk earlier.*

She closed her eyes and smiled, every vestige of fatigue and disappointment evaporating in the warmth flooding through her. "Lying on my back, staring at the ceiling. What are you doing?"

"Staring at a bottle of good red wine and wishing I had someone to share it with." His tone dropped half an octave, enslaving her further. "Interested in helping me out...again?"

"Maybe," she allowed, knowing full well there was no *maybe* about it. There might be some women who didn't succumb to icy chills and hot flushes when they found themselves on the receiving end of an unbelievable sexy baritone speaking fluent, Americanized English flavored with a dark, melodic Italian accent, but she wasn't one of them.

"If I throw in a potluck dinner, would that be enough of a bribe to persuade you?"

A deep, primitive longing clutched at her insides. "It depends. Do I have to dress...*up,* I mean?"

"Dress down," he practically purred, sending tiny shocks of awareness throbbing in her ear. "It's a casual affair."

At this rate, she'd soon need another bath! Nothing about Demetrio Bertoluzzi could ever be considered casual. He was too charismatic, too sexy, and the thought of sharing dinner with him gave her palpitations.

She pressed a fist to her racing heart. "What time?"

"How long will it take you to get ready?"

The bedside clock showed ten after six. "An hour."

Liar! She could be ready in five minutes.

"See you at seven," he said, and hung up.

No *goodbye*.

And *that,* she decided, was a very good omen.

He intercepted her the minute she stepped though her grandmother's gates to the road, emerging from the shadows so stealthily that she let out a tiny scream of shock.

"Sorry," he said. "I didn't mean to startle you."

"Well, you did, whether you meant to or not!" Her eyes were huge and luminous in the gloom. "What are you doing, lurking around out here, instead of slaving over the dinner you promised me?"

"It's pretty dark out."

Relieved laughter ran through her voice like quicksilver. "So what? You live just next door, Demetrio. I hardly think I'd have lost my way."

He caught her lightly by the wrist. Her pulse still fluttered with fear. "Maybe not, but it's a ten-minute walk down a deserted road from your place to mine."

"It's also a very *safe* deserted road."

"Perhaps." He shrugged. "But I'm in the habit of collecting my date, not expecting her to find her own way, and since I could hardly march up to your grandmother's front door and announce myself openly, I chose the next best option."

A partial truth only, delivered smoothly enough that she didn't question it, but there was no fooling himself. Cattanasca's slimy presence that afternoon, and the implicit threat in his behavior, had rattled Demetrio more than he cared to admit. Although logic dictated the man posed no immediate danger to Natalie, the fact that he'd once been a drinking buddy of Ovidio Bertoluzzi's was enough to render him suspect.

"You'd have been safe enough ringing the doorbell tonight," she said. "My grandmother's not home."

"I'm not afraid of your grandmother. I'll brave her wrath any day of the week, if that's the way you want to play it. I didn't want to cause you embarrassment, that's all."

She tipped her head to one side thoughtfully. "I don't find you embarrassing, Demetrio, but it's probably best that we remain discreet. There's no point in provoking unnecessary comment."

"Then if we're to continue meeting like this—and God help me, it seems we can't stay away from one another—we need to find a more convenient way of going about it. How do you think Grandmama would take to the idea of a connecting gate between our properties?"

He was half joking, but Natalie seized on the idea with flattering enthusiasm. "I haven't the faintest idea, nor do I propose to find out. Just go ahead and build one. The grounds are so vast, she probably won't even notice."

"And if she does?"

She leaned into him with a bewitching smile. "Sometimes, it's smarter to beg forgiveness than ask permission."

He was about to respond when the tranquility of the evening was suddenly disturbed by the sound of a car shifting gears as it left the highway and turned onto the private road accessing the waterfront properties. A few seconds later, its headlights swept in a dazzling blur over the walls fronting the Villa Rosamunda.

Without a second's hesitation, Demetrio pulled her deep into the black shadow of the nearest tree and, pressing her to the trunk, shielded her with his body.

"What're you doing?"

Her question flickered with alarm, and he cursed himself again for the weakness he hadn't been able to withstand. He'd tried convincing himself that the naked hurt he'd glimpsed in her eyes when he'd dismissed her that afternoon was the reason he'd asked her to join him for dinner. But he'd recognized his motives for the self-indulgence they really were, and a dozen times or more, he'd taken out his cell phone to call her back and cancel what any fool knew had to be a lousy idea.

So what if he'd wounded her with his surly dismissal? She'd recover, probably a lot sooner than he liked to think, and there was no question but that she'd be better off not knowing him. He knew he'd been targeted by Cattanasca, and promoting a relationship with her made her a target also. Yet when it came right down to placing that second call, the self-discipline which had pulled him back from the brink of disaster in his late teens, deserted him.

"Just being cautious," he said, tight with a fury directed entirely at himself as the car roared past without slowing. "If that had been your grandmother returning home, I didn't fancy being mown down by her car when she caught me making out with her precious granddaughter."

She let out a slow breath of relief and slid her arms around his waist. "Is that what we're doing?" she murmured on a soft laugh, her breasts brushing his chest and her hips nesting between his spread thighs.

So excruciatingly conscious of her sweet body pressed up against his that he could scarcely breathe, he said, "It probably seems that way to an onlooker."

"How does it seem to you, Demetrio?"

He was debating the best way to answer that when a pitiful howl split the night. Natalie stiffened and pulled away from him. "Was that your puppy we just heard?"

"Sounded like it," he admitted.

"Well, my goodness, what if he followed you and is out here on the road?"

"No chance of that. I left him penned up in the kitchen. He's just letting us know he doesn't appreciate being left alone."

"He could have escaped. Come *on,* Demetrio! Let's make sure he's safe."

Grabbing his hand, she tried tugging him down the road. A futile effort on her part, had he chosen to resist, since he outweighed her by at least sixty pounds. But she had a point. The pup was a wiry little thing and might have managed to squirm free of the enclosure he'd rigged up. After everything he'd done to keep it alive this far, he didn't relish the thought of it disappearing into the countryside, never to be seen again.

When they stepped into his kitchen, though, everything was just as he'd left it. The dog was still in his pen, sad-eyed, droopy-eared and unharmed. "See? What did I tell you? The mutt's fine."

"Well, I don't know about that." She crossed to the pen and scooped the pup into her arms. "This is a pretty unhappy baby, if you ask me. I think he missed you. Did you remember to feed him dinner?"

"Right after you left, princess. He ate every last bite of the stuff you brought over, and then some. And before you ask, I'm taking him to be checked out at a pet clinic in Positano tomorrow."

She kissed the dog's ears, rubbed her cheek against its head, and crooned, "You had a rough start, sweetie pie, but life's going to be pretty good from here on."

Life's pretty damn good for him already, the way you're practically drooling all over him!

Caught squarely between envy and amusement, Demetrio cleared his throat. "I hate to break up a budding love affair, but unless you want him piddling all over you again, he should probably be put outside."

"I'll go with him."

"No," he said, stuffing the corkscrew in his pocket, and collecting the wine and glasses. "We'll both go. We'll toast the full moon from the top of the cliff. And just for the record, princess, I refuse to own a dog called sweetie pie."

"Well, what are you going to call him, then?"

He took a large flashlight from the top of the refrigerator. "I don't know what's wrong with 'Mutt,'" he said, aiming a beam of light along a flagstone path running diagonally from the kitchen to the far corner of the back garden. "On the other hand, 'Mangy Mutt' has a nice ring to it. What do you think?"

"That you're seriously in need of help, in more ways than one." She laughed, relieving him of the wineglasses which were in danger of slipping out of his hand. "How about Prince, or Baron, or King?"

"For that scruffy bundle of fur? You've got to be kidding!"

They bickered amiably the rest of the way, agreeing just as they arrived at the wall separating the garden from the steep line of the cliff, that "Pippo" was a name they could both live with.

Shining the flashlight on a promontory formed by a great slab of flat rock, he illuminated an old stone bench facing the sea. "Have a seat over there, and I'll uncork the wine."

She picked her way through the tangle of weeds and ran the flat of her hand over the bench, which he knew would still be warm from the day's sun. "Oh, this is nice!" she cooed, and eyed him mischievously. "Tell me you arranged it just for me."

"Afraid not. This was my grandmother's special place. She came here often to watch the sun set, or the moon rise, and it occurred to me that you might enjoy it, too."

A smile flitted over her mouth and she fanned her full pink skirt around her like the petals of a flower. "You occurred right," she teased, every inch her royal highness perched on her throne.

He poured the wine, anchored the bottle and the flashlight firmly among the vines climbing over the wall and joined her on the bench. "Glad you approve. *Salute!*"

She touched the rim of her glass to his, her expression suddenly grave. "Thank you for bringing me here, Demetrio. I'm very honored to share such a special place with you."

Again, emotion rose up to clog his throat. Her charm and grace registered so far beyond perfect, they were off the scale. His grandmother would have adored her. "The pleasure's all mine, princess."

She sighed contentedly, and lifted her face to gaze up at the stars. "I love the scent of a garden at night, especially along this stretch of the coast, with all the jasmine and citrus groves." When he didn't answer, she angled a dreamy glance his way. "Why don't we eat dinner out here? It's so romantic, and we could use the top of the wall as a table."

"Romantic, my left foot! There are lizards and snakes living in the cracks of that wall, not to mention spiders."

She let out a little shriek. "I *hate* spiders. As for snakes…" She shuddered with distaste. "Do you realize that the day you found me stealing water in your kitchen, I climbed over that wall? Sat astride it, winded, for a good five minutes—and I was wearing nothing but shorts?"

"I know," he said, wondering how his arm had ended up around her shoulders. "Maybe you'll be more careful where you venture in future."

The heat of her body mingled with his. The subtle hint of perfume on her skin filled his senses. His arm slipped down to her waist. Barely breathing, she allowed him to draw her closer.

The result was more than either of them bargained for. An electrically charged silence scorched conversation into oblivion, along with the easy camaraderie that had carried them this far.

Stiff as boards, they sat there like a couple of teenagers desperately pretending they were completely unaware of the sexual tension sparking between them. Yet for all that he appeared engrossed in the puppy's antics as it leaped at a moth fluttering around the flashlight, in fact he was really watching her.

"Another euro for your thoughts, Demetrio," she said, not even looking his way. "What's on your mind this time?"

"You, princess."

She sighed and drew away from him. "I thought as much. You're sorry you asked me over, aren't you?"

Was he? "Yes," he said bluntly.

"Then why did you?"

"I couldn't help myself."

"But now that I'm here, you don't know what to do with me."

He raised his eyebrows and glanced out across the midnight-blue sea, praying to resist temptation. "I think you know what I'd like to do with you."

"I think I do, too. So instead of fighting it, why don't we just get on with it?"

He shot out of his seat as if he'd been stung on the behind, and paced restlessly to the wall. "Because we'd be crazy even to consider it."

It, it, it! Why were they tossing that word back and forth, when they both knew they were talking about raw, uninhibited sex?

"There's really nothing crazy about consenting adults following their natural urges."

"In our case, there is," he said. "Your family, mine…we're from different worlds, Natalie. Your grandmother—"

Rising, she went to him, took his glass and placed it with

her own on the wall. "Demetrio," she said softly, winding her arms around his neck, "this isn't about my grandmother, it's about you and me. So will you please stop looking for excuses, and just kiss me again?"

CHAPTER SEVEN

"DEFINITELY not," he said, recoiling. "That's the worst thing I could do."

But she leaned against him, and he did it anyway. With a groan that seemed to tear him apart, he framed her face in his hands and brought his mouth down on hers in a searing, volatile explosion of passion. And suddenly they weren't two rational people skirting the pitfalls of an unwise relationship, but a man and a woman so desperately hungry for one another that time and place and social mores ceased to have meaning.

He left razor burns beside her mouth, along her jaw. His callused hands rasped faintly as they slid down her throat and pushed aside the low-cut neck of her dress.

They were the sweetest sounds, the sweetest pain she'd ever known. But they weren't enough to sate the hunger driving her. She was melting inside. Pooling with heat. Ravenous.

She slid her arms around his waist. Tilted her hips against him, and reveled in the hard thrust of his erection against her pubic bone, the harsh labor of his breath against her neck.

His thumb slid inside her strapless bra to the tender slope of her breast. An inch lower, and he found her nipple, already taut with arousal, and toyed with it until she thought she'd scream in exquisite agony.

Shaking with need, she slipped her hands from his waist to his lean, taut buttocks, and let them remain there, possessing him with unadorned intimacy, something she'd ordinarily have found shockingly brazen.

But there was nothing ordinary about the moment; nothing ordinary about him. He was the most extraordinary man she'd ever met, and she wanted to know all of him, both inside and out.

Pivoting, he propped himself against the wall and, grasping her at the waist, lifted her clear off the ground so that she straddled him. The full skirt of her dress fell back, exposing her thighs and the narrow swath of fabric between her legs.

Muttering a stream of impassioned Italian, he touched her there, his hand curving against her, shaping her, pressing in just the right place to chase away any thought of snakes or lizards or spiders, and instead rendering her mindless with pleasure.

Tiny involuntary shudders swept through her, frightening because they clutched at her without mercy and she was helpless to resist them. A fierce, unexpectedly sensual side to her nature had taken charge; one consumed only with satisfying the coiling tension screaming for release deep within her.

Desperate to accommodate it, she angled herself so that Demetrio could slip his finger inside her panties. *Inside her.*

He gave a low growl of satisfaction. Cupped the back of her head with one hand, and moved his mouth over hers. Swept his tongue between her lips at the same time that, with his other hand, he stroked and cajoled the slick folds of the flesh at her core.

It was more than she'd ever hoped for from him, yet still it wasn't enough. She wanted all of him. Wanted to absorb him through every pore.

Wanted to feel him moving, naked, against her.

Wanted to feel him shudder and groan and lose control. Wanted to feel him climax in a scalding rush of heat inside her.

Wanted it all so badly that she started to cry, because he was pushing her over the edge of the world, but he wasn't coming with her. She was breaking into a thousand shimmering fragments of ecstasy, and she was doing it alone.

"Demetrio!" she gasped, clawing at his shirt until the buttons popped, then raking her nails feverishly down his bare chest, past his belt buckle to his fly.

Even through the fabric of his trousers, he was hot to the touch; burning for her, as she burned for him. But she was all thumbs as she tried to wrestle his zipper open, and conscience seized those wasted seconds to rear its untimely head and give her pause.

How easy it would be, to drown in the cool blue depths of his eyes; to melt under him and live just for this precious moment. But what about later? What about tomorrow, and next week, and next month, and the rest of her life?

Speak before it's too late, common decency urged, *because while you might be able to live with the consequences of what you're about to let happen, he might not. And if he can't, you'll lose him forever. You've heard about men not respecting women, the morning after. Well, now you're face-to-face with the very real likelihood of experiencing it firsthand!*

Wrestling herself back from the brink, she stilled her hands and lifted her face to his. "Demetrio," she gasped, trapping his hand between her legs because, left to its own devices, it would continue wreaking sensual havoc far beyond her ability to withstand, "there's something I have to tell you, before we take this any further."

"What?" he asked thickly. "That you're not protected?"

"Not that."

"Then what? You want me to stop?"

"Never! But I…I…" The words jammed in her throat, refusing to budge—temptation of the worst kind because to say nothing more spoke of tacit consent, and her treacherous body was all for that. But her mind, her brain, her damnable conscience all clamored for honesty and would not be silent.

She swallowed and tried again, blurting out her confession before she lost her courage. "I just think you ought to know that…I'm a virgin."

The last words exploded from her mouth like gunfire, and it seemed to take him a moment to grasp their meaning because, at first, he neither moved nor spoke. Grew so utterly still, in fact, that he might as well have been shot. Then, with excruciating care, he freed his hand, pulled her skirt down to cover her knees and said tightly, "Now that's a serious problem for me, princess, because I can't remember a time when I was. Which is why this has to stop, here and now."

"No, it doesn't," she practically moaned. "Not as long as you don't mind that it's the first time for me."

He slid her off his lap savagely enough that she almost fell because her legs were shaking so badly. "I mind," he ground out, his jaw rigid. "I've got enough strikes against me, without adding the sin of deflowering you to the list."

A tidal wave of loss washed over her, so intense that the tears welled up again. She had come *this* close to heaven, only to have it snatched away at the last minute by her misplaced scruples. "It's not a sin if it's what we both want," she wept. "And oh, Demetrio, I *do* want you!"

"Try telling yourself that when the kind of man you should be offering yourself to comes along, and you can hardly look yourself in the mirror because you're ashamed to know you've already squandered yourself on someone like me."

"What if *you're* the right man?"

His laugh echoed through the night, harsh and disbelieving. "Not me, princess. Not in a million years!"

"How do you know that?" she persisted. "Demetrio, I think I'm falling in love with you. I have been from the minute you came into my life."

Dear heaven, if driving him away was what she wanted, she'd surely accomplished it by uttering such words aloud! But truth cut both ways, and this admission would no more remain unspoken than the revelation of her virginity.

That she'd shocked him again was immediately apparent. He turned his face aside. Shook his head slightly. Closed his eyes and exhaled a long, shuddering breath.

Finally he looked at her and said, "You don't know what you're talking about. I can count on one hand the number of hours we've spent together. Not days, or weeks, or months, princess, but *hours!* How the devil can you seriously believe it's possible to fall in love with *anyone* in that short a time, let alone with a man like me?"

"Sometimes, a person needs only minutes to look into her heart and see the truth."

He cursed, and shoving himself away from the wall, paused just long enough to fling a parting comment over his shoulder before he headed back to the house. "Haven't you heard a word I've said? I already told you, you and I, we're oil and water, and never meant to mix."

Miserable, she watched him leave. As if sensing her distress, Pippo pawed at her knees, whimpering. Stooping, she gathered him into her arms and buried her face against his warm little body. "I don't believe him," she whispered. "I don't care what he says, I'm in love with both of you. I can't help myself."

The pup lifted its head and licked her face enthusiastically. At least *he* didn't think she was crazy.

* * *

Swearing furiously, Demetrio strode into the kitchen, his breathing labored, his body as drenched in sweat as if he'd just run a marathon. Apart from the pitiful fact that he obviously kept them well below his belt, where the *hell* were his brains that he'd allowed matters to run so dangerously close to outright disaster?

In his defense, though, a man would have had to be dead not to respond to so alluring a temptress, and he wasn't sure even death would have proved sufficient deterrent. Her breasts had been cool and firm to his touch, her nipples tight little buds blooming against his fingertips, her inner thighs smooth as cream, her womanhood warm and sweet and soft as velvet.

He blinked as a fresh burst of sweat broke out on his face. Every inch of her, from head to foot, was delectable enough to make a monk think twice about taking vows of chastity, and anyone less suited to monkhood than Demetrio Bertoluzzi didn't exist.

As for the mayhem she'd wrought with her hands, tracing delicate patterns over his biceps, shaping the curve of muscle at his shoulder, fluttering uncertainly at his groin…! Hell, just thinking about it left him rock-hard and close to exploding, and not because she was such an expert lover—he'd had enough of them to know the difference—but because she'd been so artless in her explorations.

Everything about her had been so scrupulously honest, she'd made his heart swell. He wasn't used to that, and he didn't have the first idea how to deal with it. It had been all he could do, not to run from her as fast and as far as he could go.

Problem was, a man could never escape from himself. At the end of the race, the troubles were right behind him, a shadow he could never outrun, and sooner or later, he had to deal with them.

Uncertain footsteps approaching from the garden told him that, in this case, it was going to be sooner. She wasn't about to disappear into the night and leave him in peace, and he'd have been a born fool to believe otherwise. Burying a sigh, he turned to face her.

"I brought Pippo home," she said, sounding so subdued that he bled for her. "I didn't think you'd want him left outside to roam. But that's the only reason I'm here. I know you want me gone."

Yeah, he wanted her gone. But more than that, he wanted her, and not just in his bed. He wanted to make her smile and hear her laugh. Wanted to watch her across the table and learn more about her, as they shared the simple dinner he'd planned. Even wanted to share something of his own history with her, and that was a first for him.

Still, for both their sakes, getting rid of her was the wisest course. So how the blazes did he wind up saying, "You might as well stay. You have to eat, after all, and there's enough here for two."

The tip of her tongue peeked out and swept nervously over her upper lip. "You're just being polite."

"Well, why not, princess? Good manners aren't just the prerogative of the well-bred rich, you know."

"I didn't mean to imply they were!" she exclaimed, flushing delectably.

"Then stop hovering in the doorway, and have another glass of wine while I throw together a meal for us."

She approached, eyeing him as warily as if he'd suggested she perform a striptease on the table. "You can cook?"

"Yes," he said, opening another bottle of wine and pouring it into fresh glasses because, in his haste to escape her, he'd left the others on the cliff wall. "Why does that surprise you?"

"Because most men I know can't boil water. What are you making?"

"Pasta alla carbonara, Bertoluzzi-style. Not exactly a local specialty, but..."

Busy hauling supplies out of the refrigerator and the food safe he'd rigged up in the old walk-in pantry, he let the sentence drift into silence.

Misunderstanding, she said, "But it's the one dish you can do well?"

He assembled everything he needed for the main course: eggs, lean slices of pancetta, pecorino cheese, a loaf of ciabatta bread, pasta made fresh that morning from a shop in Positano and tomatoes he'd bought from a vendor on the side of the road. "Not in the least," he said smugly. "I'm Italian. I don't know how to cook badly."

Setting the dog to run loose on the floor, she perched on a stool on the other side of the table and picked up her wineglass. "You might be Italian but, as I've mentioned before, there's a hint of an American accent in your English. How is that?"

"My mother was American. She met my father when she came here on holiday, and married him within the month. After he died, she moved back to the States and took me with her. I was four at the time."

"Oh, Demetrio!" Her beautiful gray eyes grew wide with distress. "How tragic for her to be widowed so young, and for you to grow up without a father."

He adjusted the flame under a heavy cast-iron frying pan and threw in a dollop of olive oil. While it heated, he cut up the pancetta and smashed a clove of garlic with the flat side of an old chef's knife. "In your world, perhaps, but not in mine," he informed her, mincing the garlic and tossing it and the pancetta in the pan. "My father died a mobster's death, shot down in the street in broad daylight, and I'm willing to bet my mother didn't waste a single tear on him. From what I later learned, theirs was a marriage made closer to hell than heaven, and she never felt at home here."

"I can see why she left, then. And I suppose, too, that she wanted to put distance between you and such terrible happenings."

"She wanted a fresh start, and she found one." He whisked eggs in a bowl, added the grated pecorino, and wielded the pepper grinder over the mix with a good deal more energy than it required as an old, familiar sense of injustice rose up in him. "Unfortunately I wasn't part of it. Pass me that jar of salt, will you?"

"What do you mean, you weren't part of it?" Shoving over the salt, Natalie stared at him, a frown puckering the smooth skin of her forehead. "Surely you're not saying she abandoned you?"

"Not right away." The pancetta was crisp and lightly browned. Removing it from the stove, he tossed it in with the eggs, turned up the heat under a pot of water he'd left simmering on the second burner, added a spoonful of the coarse salt, and when the water came to a boil, threw in the pasta. "She remarried just after my sixth birthday, and when the new husband decided he didn't want to be saddled with a gangster's brat, she sent me back here to live with my father's parents."

She sucked in a shocked breath. "How could a mother do that to a little boy—to her only child?"

"Beats me." He shrugged. "But I didn't care. My grandmother was all the mother I needed. When she died…"

He stopped, stabbed by an unexpected pang of grief. She'd been gone nearly fifteen years, and he thought he'd recovered from her loss, but she'd been much in his thoughts since he'd come back to the villa. He saw her in her garden, tending her

The Harlequin Reader Service® — Here's How It Works:

Accepting your 2 free Harlequin Presents® larger print books and 2 free gifts places you under no obligation to buy anything. You may keep the books and gifts and return the shipping statement marked "cancel." If you do not cancel, about a month later we'll send you 6 additional Harlequin Presents larger print books and bill you just $4.05 each in the U.S. or $4.72 each in Canada, plus 25¢ shipping & handling per book and applicable taxes if any.* That's the complete price and — compared to cover prices of $4.75 each in the U.S. and $5.75 each in Canada — it's quite a bargain! You may cancel at any time, but if you choose to continue, every month we'll send you 6 more books, which you may either purchase at the discount price or return to us and cancel your subscription.

Terms and prices subject to change without notice. Sales tax applicable in N.Y. Canadian residents will be charged applicable provincial taxes and GST. All orders subject to approval. Credit or debit balances in a customer's account(s) may be offset by any other outstanding balance owed by or to the customer. Please allow 4 to 6 weeks for delivery.

ACTUAL TYPE SIZE!

Would you like to read Harlequin Presents® novels with larger print?

Larger Print Editions

GET 2 FREE LARGER PRINT BOOKS!

Harlequin Presents® novels are now available in a larger print edition! These books are complete and unabridged, but the type is larger, so it's easier on your eyes.

YES! Please send me 2 FREE *Harlequin Presents* novels in the larger print format and 2 FREE mystery gifts! I understand I am under no obligation to purchase any books as explained on the back of this card.

376 HDL ELYF   176 HDL EL2F

FIRST NAME   LAST NAME

ADDRESS

APT #   CITY

STATE/PROV.   ZIP/POSTAL CODE

Order online at:
www.eHarlequin.com

HLP-P-05/07

beloved roses. Heard her crooning to him as he fell asleep in the bed she had waiting for him when he landed on her doorstep, a waif with a suitcase containing a few clothes and a beaten-up old teddy bear. Even caught a faded whiff of her perfume in the clothes closet of the master suite.

"Yes?" Natalie prompted, her voice soft with sympathy. "What happened after that?"

He'd cried for a week, the first tears he'd shed since his mother had walked away and left an Alitalia flight attendant to escort him on the long trip back to Italy. And damn it, Natalie's gentle concern was bringing him disastrously close to doing the same thing again now. Bad enough that she had his hormones in a riot, but that she was scratching away at his well-armored emotions and leaving them dented and scarred, was insufferable.

The pasta was done. Glad of an excuse to turn away from her, he lifted the pot off the stove, drained it at the sink, and busied himself tossing the pancetta and egg combination into the hot noodles. Unasked, she made herself useful laying out the cutlery and bowls he'd piled at the end of the table, and ripping paper towels from the roll above the sink.

"Paper towels for napkins, and thick pottery instead of fine china? Not exactly what you're used to, is it, princess?" he remarked dryly, slicing the ciabatta onto a wooden board.

"Stop trying so hard to be boorish," she said. "Once you've restored your dining room, we'll go out and buy all the fine china and crystal your heart desires, and celebrate in style."

"I doubt you'll still be here when that happens."

She almost snorted with derision, except she was too much of a lady to carry it off. "You're not getting rid of me that easily, Demetrio. I'm not going anywhere, anytime soon."

Her last remark gave him the opening to ask a question he'd been mulling over ever since the day she'd arrived. "Exactly how long is it that you expect to be here?"

"The rest of the summer."

"To do what?"

"Nothing. I'm on holiday—the first I've taken in ove
three years."

In other words, she'd be a constant source of irritation, distraction and virginal temptation for the next three months
Terrific! Just what he needed!

She took a tomato from the bowl and cradled it tenderly
in the palm of her hand. "These are the reddest, most deli-
cious-looking tomatoes I've ever seen. What are you going
to do with them?"

"Slice and serve them as is, drizzled with olive oil and
balsamic vinegar," he snarled, wondering if she had the first idea
how sensuous he found her actions. The way she was caress-
ing that tomato, stroking one finger over its glossy skin, lifting
it to inhale its scent, left him almost crippled with arousal.

She plopped it back in the bowl, and he winced. "Give me
a knife, and I'll take care of that while you dish up the carbonara," she said.

Forcing his mind out of the gutter, he passed over the
chef's knife. "For a woman who grew up with servants
catering to her every whim, you're probably no more experi-
enced at this than you are at gardening. Try not to take the
end off your fingers while you're at it, okay?"

She laughed, and again he had to turn away. The alluring
shape of her mouth, the sparkle in her eyes, the creamy
elegance of her throat when she tilted her head back, threatened his control unmercifully.

"Don't take all night," he said, shoving a shallow dish and a
cruet of oil and vinegar toward her. "The pasta's ready to serve."

She'd dined by candlelight in the world's most famous restaurants, in the world's most beautiful cities, as the guest of

diplomats, minor royalty, and heads of state. Eaten meals prepared by chefs of international repute. And never had she been more thoroughly seduced than she was that night, with Demetrio, in the vast, ugly old kitchen, with a slab of plywood for a table and a simple pasta dish for a main course.

It was all his fault. If he'd left the naked lightbulb burning, she wouldn't have found herself cocooned with him in a warm, golden circle of candle flame that shrank the rest of the room to a shifting palette of shadows. The wine wouldn't have glimmered like priceless rubies, or tasted like nectar from heaven. His eyes wouldn't have mated with hers in a flickering tango of advance and retreat. Their voices wouldn't have fallen to husky whispers as they exchanged snippets of personal history.

"I loved school," she told him.

"I hated it," he said.

"Every day was full of promise," she reminisced. "I fell asleep every night dreaming of tomorrow."

"I never slept deeply enough to shut out the nightmares."

She reached across the table. Wrapped her fingers around his. "What kind of nightmares?"

"The kind that don't evaporate in the clear light of day." His eyes grew anguished, his mouth grim. "One night in particular I remember as if it happened just yesterday. I was awakened by the hopeless cries of some poor young woman pleading with my grandfather for her husband's life. I crept from my room and watched from the minstrel's gallery.

"She was no more than twenty, on her knees at my grandfather's feet, and hugely pregnant, although at the time I thought she was just fat. Her husband stood to one side, hands bound behind him, his face ashen. 'I carry his baby,' she wept. 'You have a family of your own, Don Bertoluzzi. You know what it is to love. How can you deny this unborn child the right to know his father?'"

Natalie froze, the pain in his voice pebbling her skin with goose bumps. "What happened?"

He fetched a third bottle of wine from the pantry, uncorked it and poured them both another glass. "Her pleas fell on deaf ears. Unmoved, my grandfather nodded once, then stood by as, out of the shadows, his 'aides' appeared, dragged her husband outside, shoveled him into a waiting car and drove him away."

He stared into his untouched wine and sank into a silence tormented by memories she could never, in her wildest dreams, begin to comprehend. She'd been surrounded by the safety and love and security of family her entire life. The kind of violence he'd witnessed had never even come close to touching her.

"I never knew what crime the man supposedly committed," he finally went on, "but his face as he turned for one last look at his wife, the hopelessness in his eyes, the utter devastation in hers, haunted my dreams for months afterward."

Unutterably moved, Natalie said, "Demetrio, I'm so sorry you had to witness something so frightful. How old were you?"

"Seven or eight—I'm not exactly sure."

"Dear God! If only your grandmother had known—"

"She did," he said. "She found me crouched in the gallery. I don't know how—maybe I made some sound, maybe she went to check on me before going to bed herself—but I remember her coming from her upstairs sitting room and carrying me to my bed. She stayed with me until I fell asleep. The next day, it was as if nothing untoward had ever happened. She never referred to the incident again, and neither did I."

"Why didn't she take you and leave that monster of a husband?"

"Because she knew he would never let her go, and if she

tried, he'd find ways to punish her that you can't begin to imagine."

Was it the utter desolation she saw on his face that drove her to that next, irreversible step? The urgent need to wipe the emptiness from his eyes and fill him with hope and warmth and belief in the goodness of life? Perhaps. Or perhaps she simply knew, with unerring female insight, that only a woman's love could erase the lingering horror in his mind.

"Let's go upstairs, Demetrio," she murmured, drawing him away from the table. "Show me the rest of the house."

"I don't think so, princess," he said. "That doesn't strike me as a good idea at all."

But she pulled his head down and brought his mouth to hers and kissed him. She heard his breathing grow labored. She felt the accelerated throb of the pulse at the side of his neck, felt the resistance seeping out of him, and the rising heat of passion driving away the ghosts.

"Trust me, it's the best idea in the world," she whispered, and somehow, they found themselves traversing the passage to the grand hall, then up the branched staircase, and along the landing to the room he'd occupied as a child and where he slept still. She knew this because his clothes hung in the open wardrobe, and there were sheets and pillows, and an old, exquisitely worked quilt on the bed. A reading lamp stood on the nightstand, with an open book lying facedown next to it. And the casement windows stood open to the mild, starlit night.

As bedrooms went, it was stark and bare, but it was his, and being in it with him charged the atmosphere with heightened awareness. Just as the candles had reduced the kitchen to a warm, spotlit circle inviting shared confidences, so did the close confines of his room cradle them in intimacy. How could they not, with the bed luring her to test its single mattress and draw him down beside her?

"This hardly looks big enough for a man your size," she said.

"It serves the purpose, for now."

"I don't know how." Knowing she was tempting him cruelly, she stretched out with her head on the pillow and her arms spread wide. "Look, even I barely fit."

But he wouldn't look. Instead he turned his head and stared out the window. "Get off the bed, princess," he said, in a strangled voice. "I know what you're doing, and it's not going to work."

Inching closer to the edge, she caught his hand and tugged. He spun toward her, his eyes glowing with blue fire. "I mean it, Natalie! Cut it out!"

"Why?" she whispered. "You know that's why you brought me up here to begin with, and you know it's what we both want."

"That doesn't make it right."

She brought his hand to her mouth. Unfolded his fingers and circled his palm with her tongue—an untaught, instinctive gesture that brought him tumbling down next to her with a groan of defeat. Then his mouth was on hers, in a kiss so hot and hungry that she melted from the middle out.

His teeth tugged gently at her lips. His tongue delved deep. Stole her breath. Stole her heart.

Fingers of heat licked over her body, knotted between her thighs. She tunneled her fingers through his hair, sighed his name into his mouth, tilted her pelvis to nest against his.

A sheen of sweat gleamed on his forehead. "Witch!" he ground out hoarsely, dragging his mouth away from hers and forcibly holding her at arm's length when she'd tried to cling to him. "Get up and go home, before I forget I'm trying to do the honorable thing."

So far beyond shame or modesty that she could barely recall what the words even meant, she whispered, "No. I want to be with you. Please, Demetrio, don't send me away. We need each other tonight."

"Not like this—not with your mind clouded by wine," he insisted.

But she was drunk on desire, not wine. Intoxicated by all that had preceded the moment—not just the kisses, the caresses, the near-intimacy and muttered endearments he hadn't been able to suppress in the garden, at a place so dear to the heart of the grandmother he both revered and cherished, but because, for the first time, he'd shared something of himself without her having to drag it out of him, one syllable at a time.

In allowing her glimpses of his past, he'd revealed a vulnerability she'd never suspected. And with every word, every glance, he'd wormed his way more thoroughly into her heart.

They'd come too far in a few short hours for her to let it end there. Resolutely, she climbed off the bed, removed her dress, and dropped it on the floor. Her bra followed, then her panties until she stood before him without a stitch of clothing to hide her nakedness.

"My mind has never been clearer, Demetrio," she said.

He reared up on one elbow, his eyes sliding in stunned disbelief from her body to her face, and back again. "What the hell do you think you're doing?"

She climbed astride him. Kissed him on the mouth again. Brushed her nipples over his chest. Took his hand and guided it between her legs. "Showing you how much I want to make love," she said. "So are you going to take your clothes off, or shall I do it for you?"

CHAPTER EIGHT

HE SCRUNCHED his eyes shut and groaned. She stroked his cheek. Whispered into his mouth, "It'll be all right."

He wrenched his face aside. "It'll be the biggest mistake of both our lives."

She unbuttoned his shirt and kissed his chest. Swirled her tongue over his nipples and in the dip of his navel. "Does this feel like a mistake, Demetrio?" she murmured, then slid lower and pressed her mouth against the fabric of his trousers where it stretched taut over his erection. "Does this?"

He shuddered. "For God's sake, Natalie …!"

She opened his fly and released him. Stared, spellbound, and ran her fingers lightly over him. He was big, so much bigger than she expected. So hard and smooth. So utterly perfect.

He uttered a sound low in his throat, a choking growl of sorts, and lunged off the bed so abruptly that he sent the lamp on the nightstand crashing to the floor. His clothes went sailing across the room, and he turned to her, his eyes wild, his face flushed, his chest heaving.

Then they were tumbling together in a tangle of limbs and searching hands, and frantic, hungry kisses, on the too-short, too-narrow bed of his youth. At one point, he panted, "This is insane, princess!"

"Is it, my love?"

He shook his head. "No," he said, and pushed her onto her back.

She opened herself to him—her arms, her legs, her heart, her soul. He straddled her, nudged the tip of his penis against her, then slid it between the folds of her flesh.

The breath caught in her throat and she whispered his name.

He braced himself on his elbows, and stared into her eyes. "I don't want to hurt you, princess."

"You won't," she said, a tide of sensation swelling within her.

"Are you sure?"

"More sure than anything I've ever known."

Still supporting his weight, he pressed harder, slid deeper. She tensed as a brief, sharp sliver of discomfort clutched at her.

He froze, his gaze searching her face. "Do you want me to stop?"

The blind, agonizing need in his eyes matched that thundering through her blood. "Not in a million years."

He clenched his jaw, drove a little harder, then harder still until he filled her completely. "Princess?"

She smiled and pulled him down until his body covered hers. "If you dare stop now, I'll die."

He brought his mouth to hers again and rocked slowly against her. She caught his rhythm, and moved with him as naturally, as easily, as if they'd been rehearsing for years, for just that moment.

Gradually the tempo increased, lost its measured beat, became terrifying and thrilling in its race to bring them to completion. He caught her bottom in his hands, surged into her again and again, each thrust more peremptory than its predecessor.

She began to tremble, drawn into a primal ritual of intimacy that brought her, shattered and mindless, to teeter again on the edge of the world. But this time she was not alone. She was safe in the arms of the man she loved. He was flying beside her, reaching for the same stars, and calling her name in a voice fractured by passion.

At the last, he tensed, locked in mortal combat with a force beyond his control, then let go with a mighty groan as his body shuddered and throbbed in utter surrender.

Trapped in the same struggle, she arched beneath him, at the mercy of the elemental release bolting through her. Again and again, it exerted its power, imploding at her core with such unyielding force that her flesh clenched around him in glorious despair. "I love you!" she cried, her heart so full that she could no more have withheld the words than she could halt the shimmering spasms streaking through her.

Eventually the tumult passed, faded into diminishing stabs of sensation. An unearthly silence filled the room. He grew still. Too still. Then taking her with him, he rolled onto his back, stroked the damp hair from her forehead and muttered, "Are you all right?"

Disconcerted as much by his physical reaction as the fact that he hadn't responded in kind, she said, "Why do you ask? Is it because I said I love you, and you think I spoke in the heat of the moment and will regret it later?"

"I ask because you came to me a virgin," he said on a sigh fraught with…what? Impatience? Irritation? Regret? "Naturally I'm concerned. Any man would be. The first time can't be a very…comfortable experience."

"It was an incredible experience, and you're not just *any* man." She took his hand and rested it under the curve of her left breast. "Feel how my heart still races, Demetrio, and know that you're the reason. But be sure that my mind has never been clearer. I *do* love you."

Another silence dropped into the room like a heavy curtain

ringing down on the final scene in a play, obliterating all the beautiful warmth and intimacy they'd shared just a short time before. Even the night grew darker as the moon slid behind a tree.

"You might want to leave about now," he eventually said, in a voice so gentle that it chilled her to the bone. "Before you decide you hate me."

Again, she reached for him. "I could never hate you!"

He pushed her hands away and slid off the bed. "Go home, princess," he said, passing her her clothes before climbing into his own.

Even she, inexperienced as she was in after-intercourse protocol, recognized a brush-off when she heard one. Stifling the disappointment welling up and threatening to drown her, she dressed as speedily as dignity would allow. Together, they went down to the kitchen again, but when he made to walk her home, she stopped him with an upraised hand.

"I've survived the evening so far," she said, pride stiffening her spine as well as her voice. "I think I can make it the rest of the way by myself."

"I'd prefer to—"

"I wouldn't. Thank you for…everything."

"Princess," he began.

But he'd said enough—or not, depending on their separate points of view. He wasn't going to tell her he loved her, and there really wasn't anything else she cared to hear. "Good night, Demetrio," she managed, and stepped into the night without another word.

It was close to midnight; late enough, she thought, that she'd be able to sneak up to her room, undetected. Instead, as she let herself in through the French doors and crept silently from the terrace and through the day salon to the foyer, the front door suddenly swished open. A second later, she found herself pinned equally between the blazing lights of the chandelier suspended above the curving stairwell, and her grandmother's gimlet-eyed stare.

"I thought you'd be in bed already," she heard herself stammer, guilty as a schoolgirl caught breaking curfew.

"And I was of the impression that's where you'd spent the entire evening," Barbara replied without missing a beat. "Apparently I was mistaken. Do I dare inquire where you've been—" her gaze dropped to the incriminating evidence of the sandals dangling from Natalie's hand "—that you feel it necessary to make so stealthy a return?"

Blinded by the unforgiving glare of the chandelier, and too miserable even to try to come up with a lie, Natalie said, "You know very well where I've been, Grandmother, so let's not play games. I had dinner with Demetrio Bertoluzzi."

"Until this hour? My goodness, how many courses did he serve?"

Suppressing the urge to say that, while the main course had been delicious, the dessert served in the bedroom had both exceeded, and fallen short of her expectations, she shrugged with Oscar-winning nonchalance. "About as many as Marianna Sorrentino, I imagine, since you're only just arriving home yourself. And before you launch into another homily on the folly of my associating with Demetrio, you'll be happy to hear he agrees with you. The way we left things tonight, I doubt he'll ask me back again."

"Then I won't say another word," her grandmother declared with a grim smile. "Not even *I told you so!*"

He paced the upper floor most of that night, cursing himself for his own weakness, for the pain he knew he'd inflicted on Natalie, for the impossible situation in which he'd landed them both. And cursing her for her stubborn belief that he was worthy of her love.

He was thirty-four and had been a social outcast for more than half that time. But he was tough. He'd had to be, to survive those years under his grandfather's roof, otherwise he'd be dead by now.

Eventually he'd built a new life, found success, made friends respected for their integrity and decency. That didn't mean, however, that he'd forgotten how it felt to be on the outside, looking in. And therein lay the insurmountable difference between him and Natalie.

If he let her invade his heart—and only God knew how badly he wanted to do just that—she'd learn the hard way something he'd understood from the time he was a child: that being rejected, in her case by the society which once had embraced her, dealt a wound that never properly healed. She wouldn't survive such a blow, and he wouldn't let her push him into proving it.

He could have made it easier on both of them and explained why he was representing himself as a man with little to his name but the crumbling villa he'd inherited. But he had his pride, just as she had hers, and he'd vowed a long time ago never to apologize to anyone, ever again, for who he was. He would not hide from himself, and he wouldn't allow others to do so, either.

The people who mattered in her life had made his grandmother's miserable, and he hadn't transformed himself so far that he couldn't take a certain pleasure in making them eat crow when the time was right. She might not see it now, but by keeping her at a distance, he was doing her a favor, because when he exacted his revenge, he would cut his own throat, metaphorically, at least. Her grandmother's circle would never forgive him for making fools of them, and if she was, in their eyes, allied with him, they'd never forgive her, either.

First light was touching the sky when he found himself on

the master suite loggia. To the west, between the branches of the trees separating his property from Barbara Wade's, he could see Natalie's bedroom. Caught in the light offshore breeze, a wisp of white drapery floated light as gossamer through the open glass doors to her balcony.

He hoped she was sleeping, that she'd had a better night than he had. He hoped anger and disgust had soured her romantic illusions about him, and that she'd decided that what she'd mistakenly thought was love was really nothing more than infatuation. She was smart, educated, sophisticated. At some level, she had to be aware that it wasn't uncommon for a woman to invest the man who introduced her to sex, with a glamour he didn't deserve.

And if she didn't? "Then better a little pain now, than a load of grief later on, princess," he said, gazing at that swath of drifting drapery, and wishing he could wave a magic wand and make everything right between him and her.

Four days later, he went to City Hall in Positano to check on local permit requirements for upgrading residential plumbing. When he returned to his truck, he found the left rear tire flat. Fortunately he'd parked on a level side street.

It was the only thing going in his favor. Thoroughly ticked off, he gave the offending wheel a kick. The vehicle itself was old, but the tires were new and there was no reason that he could see for one of them to have failed. On top of that, he had to move his latest load of building supplies to get at the spare, and the heat that day was enough to kill a man.

"The imperfect ending to one hell of an imperfect week," he growled, stacking the supplies to one side, and hauling out the jack and spare. "Damned shoddy tire manufacturer!"

"Need some help?"

Glancing up, he met the sympathetic eye of a man passing

by. No more than about thirty, he wore shorts, a T-shirt and sneakers, and had a camera slung around his neck. His long dark hair, streaked blond, was tied back in a ponytail. A small silver ring hung from his left ear.

To the uninitiated, he was just another trendy tourist enjoying the sights. But Demetrio had had enough experience in his youth to recognize an undercover cop when he saw one, even if this particular member of the force wore a genial smile.

Prying off the hubcap with the lug wrench and loosening the lug bolts, he said, "I guess the minute I sign my name and people realize who I am, I become an immediate suspect around here."

His companion squatted next to him, to all intents and purposes interested only in handing him the jack. "Detective Cristofani Russo," he introduced himself in a low voice, "and in this instance, your name works both to your advantage and ours."

"How so?"

"You had a visitor the other day. A developer by the name of Cattanasca."

"Are you telling me I've been under surveillance?"

"Not you, *signor.* But Cattanasca's every movement is of great interest to us."

"Then you probably already know he wants to buy my villa."

Russo nodded. "He's wanted it for a very long time, and thought he'd eventually acquire it—until you showed up and started restoring the place."

"And you care about that because…?"

"He has plans to turn your property into a gated community of twenty town houses, and adding to his fortunes by charging a very high price for them."

"In that neighborhood?" Working swiftly to remove the

flat, Demetrio spared him a scornful glance. "Not a chance! The Residents' Association would veto it in a flash."

"You'd be surprised what Cattanasca has gotten away with over the years." Russo handed him the lug bolts as he shoved the spare in place, and proceeded to describe the kind of corrupt power the man wielded in the area.

Cattanasca was a loan shark, as well as a developer. Known for his black market dealings. Guilty of bribery to circumvent building regulations and zoning laws; of cheating uninformed owners out of the proper value of their land; of using inferior construction materials—and with enough high-ranking officials on his payroll to make it easy for him to do so without once being apprehended.

"This town deserves better than to have its reputation sullied by a man like Cattanasca," Russo concluded. "He has to be stopped, and we believe you can help us make it happen."

"Why me?" Demetrio sat back on his heels, for once caught by surprise.

"Because you're the perfect candidate for the job—a man whose family's past doesn't bear close inspection, and who's undertaken a massive renovation with no apparent way to pay for it."

"Stop right there," Demetrio snapped. "First, things aren't always as they seem. And second, not even for the police will I compromise my integrity."

"We've been very thorough in our research. We're well aware there's a great deal more to you than meets the eye, *signor,* and we're not asking you to jeopardize your principles. Your integrity is precisely what makes you the ideal man for the kind of sting we have in mind. The worst we'll ask is that you hold your nose and put up with the smell that accompanies having to deal with Cattanasca, and keep our arrangement in strict confidence."

"I came back here to make peace with myself, and force my neighbors to recognize my worth, not to start a war with them. That's hardly going to be possible if it becomes common knowledge that I'm doing business with someone like Cattanasca."

"Once we've achieved our objective, we'll publicly clear your name of any involvement with him. Naturally we'll give you our guarantee of that, in writing."

Russo paused just long enough to intimate he was saving the best for last. "Look at it this way, *signor.* From your standpoint, it's a win-win situation. Carry this off, and you'll do more than win your neighbors' respect. You'll earn their lasting gratitude and admiration, as well."

A heady prospect, but he'd learned a long time ago not to dive headfirst into a pool without first checking the depth of the water. "You still haven't told me what you want me to do."

"At this point?" Russo helped him reload his supplies in the truck bed, then shook his hand, managing to transfer a business card to Demetrio as he did so. "Take a day or two to think over what I've said. If you decide you're interested, give me a call."

"Okay, but no promises."

"I understand."

He slammed the tailgate closed. "Thanks for the help."

"Anytime." Before continuing on his way, Russo turned one last time. "Oh, and about the flat—don't blame the manufacturer. All that tire needs is to be reinflated."

"Yeah." He gave a grudging laugh. "I figured that out already."

"You're a smart man. It's one of the reasons we chose you."

Bathed in the heat of a sun tempered by the sea breeze and lulled by the distant rush of the waves, Natalie lay facedown on her towel, hovering midway between awake and asleep. A lovely, hazy state that numbed the sharp ache in her heart and left her drowsily immune to the conversation she'd had with her grandmother that morning.

"…I'm invited to a house party on Capri. Come with me, Natalie. There'll be other people your age. I'm sure you'd have a good time."

She meant well, of course, but didn't understand that, in her present fragile state, Natalie couldn't deal with Barbara's hovering concern. "Thanks, Grandmother, but I'll pass."

"Darling, this isn't healthy. You need to get out of this house."

"I do. Every day."

"Spending hours alone on the beach isn't exactly what I mean."

But it was an escape; a place where she could be alone and nurse her emotional wounds. "There's more of a breeze down there," she'd argued, which was true. The last few days, the temperature on the terrace had climbed above ninety, leaving the sheltered pool area unbearably hot. "And I actually prefer swimming in the sea."

Her grandmother had shuddered. "There are *things* in the sea, darling. *Live* things! As for climbing up and down that cliff…!"

"The exercise is good for me."

"Well, I suppose anything's better than wasting your time on that dreadful Demetrio Bertoluzzi."

Even in her present slumberous state, the memory of his name made her fingers burrow convulsively in the hot sand. "I don't want to talk about him, and if you persist in bringing him up every chance you get, I'll start sleeping on the beach, as well. Go to Capri and have a good time. I'll be fine here by myself."

She'd made her point. Her grandmother had left, and

Natalie was immersed in the peace and quiet her ravaged spirit craved. She might even fall sleep, she thought languidly—something that escaped her at night.

Murmuring a sigh, she let the relaxation steal over her limbs and the blackness fill her mind...

She was on a train open to cool, winter weather. She could hear its steam engine huffing. Could feel the sharp sting of sleet stabbing into her bare shoulders, then the sudden change to summer as the mild slap of rain washed down her cheek...

With a start, she came awake and hid her face in the towel as a shower of wet sand sprayed over her. A warm tongue investigated her ear. Sharp little nails dug into her arm, and a shrill *yip* scattered the lingering shreds of sleep. She smelled wet dog and puppy breath, and turning her head, found herself nose to nose with Pippo.

"Oh, sweetie pie!" She scrambled to her knees and caught the dog's damp little body to her. Hugged and kissed him, and didn't give a rap that he shed hair all over her. "I've missed you. How did you know where to find me?"

"Actually," Demetrio said, from somewhere behind her, "he didn't. I brought him down here."

How was it possible for ice to burn? For it to slide over her skin and leave her laboring to breathe in its heat?

She ran her tongue over lips suddenly desert-dry, and felt a sheen of perspiration dot her eyelids.

"I'm sorry," he went on. "If I'd known you were already here, I'd have—"

Not daring to turn to look at him, she shook her head. "No need to apologize. I don't own the beach."

"Even so, I wouldn't have disturbed you."

"You didn't."

"You were sleeping."

"No, I wasn't. I was about to leave." Releasing Pippo, she

scooped up her towel and sandals, sprang to her feet and spun toward the cliff. Instead she came up smack against his chest. His naked chest. Nothing new in that, though, was there? She'd never known a man with a greater aversion to wearing a shirt.

He caught her elbows, his hands warm and rough against her skin. "You're lying, princess."

"Yes, I am," she spat defiantly. "Because you don't seem able to handle the truth! Now take your hands off me and let me go."

"No."

"What?" Slack-jawed, she stared at him. The men she knew—*her* kind of men, as he was so fond of calling them—knew better than to ignore a woman when she told them to back off.

"No," he said again.

"I could have you arrested for that."

"Princess," he said, drawing her inexorably closer, until his words grazed her lips, and his dark head shut out the glare of the sun, and his bare thighs aligned themselves with hers, and his pelvis nested against her belly, "the ideas filling my head right now, and what I'm planning to do about them, could land me in jail for the next ten years. And right this minute, I don't give a rat's ass."

He kissed her then with the desperation of a drowning man gasping for air. With mind-shattering need. With a groan that seemed torn from his soul. With an intensity that rocked the ground under her feet. And because she couldn't help herself, she kissed him back.

How long they clung to one another perhaps only Pippo knew because, at last, he let out an exasperated yelp and scrabbled his paws up her leg. Cursing softly, Demetrio let her go.

She backed away from him and lifted trembling fingers to her lips. "Why did you do that?"

"Why do you think?" he said, his eyes full of torment. "Because I couldn't help myself. Because I'm a damned fool. Because you're here, and walking away from you is more than I can bring myself to do."

"Why are you a fool?"

He glanced aside, that endearing, self-deprecating little smile touching his mouth. "I sent you away, didn't I?"

"Yes," she said, around the ache in her throat.

"Well, guess what? I'm asking you to come back again."

"Why?"

He touched himself where he was thick with arousal, a quick, inexpressibly erotic gesture that turned her liquid inside. "Look at me, princess! Why do you think?"

"Because you want sex?"

"No," he said roughly. "Because I want you."

CHAPTER NINE

UNTIL that moment, he hadn't made up his mind. But holding her in his arms again, tasting the sweet wildness of her mouth, he knew he was going to take Cristofani Russo up on his proposal. He'd go to any lengths to prove himself worthy of another chance with her.

Arriving at the decision, though, didn't alleviate the moment. He was pulsing with hunger for her and, from the dazed acquiescence in her eyes and the way her breasts rose and fell in agitation, she was more than ready for him. Scaling the cliff to his house was out of the question. There was no time.

A quick glance up and down the narrow strip of beach showed it to be deserted. Grabbing her hand, he drew her to where the base of the cliff afforded them a scant measure of privacy, and tossed a rubber chew toy to the dog to keep him occupied. Then, spreading her big beach towel on the sand, he turned again to her.

She wore a lime green two-piece bathing suit. Not the kind of brief bikini other women might have chosen, but something less revealing, which made what it concealed all the more alluring. Within seconds, he stripped it away, shed his own swimming trunks, and without even a suggestion of foreplay, he pulled her down onto the towel and sank into her with an almighty groan.

He came almost at once and so, God love her, did she, rising up to meet him and locking her legs around his waist as the spasms racked her body and milked him of every last drop of seed.

For long minutes afterward, they lay together, their bodies still joined. He stroked her hair, her face. Kissed her eyelids, her nose, her jaw, her ears. Ran his hands down her throat and over her breasts. Felt her shudder beneath his fingers. And felt himself grow hard all over again.

They took it slowly, the second time. Savored every second, to touch each other, to murmur in wonder that they'd found each other again. And still it ended too soon, in a rush of heat that seared his soul.

Depleted to the point of exhaustion, he drew the end of the towel over their limbs and up around their hips, and cradled her to his chest. "I could lie here with you all night," he told her.

"I wish you would," she said. "I'd love to spend a whole night with you."

He dropped a kiss on the crown of her head. "I didn't use protection. You could be pregnant."

"Would you mind, if I was?"

"It's not something I'd be proud of, princess. I'm old enough to know better. But if you're asking me if I'd abandon you, the answer's no."

When she closed her eyes, her lashes feathered against his chest. "I'm probably not," she murmured contentedly. "My period only just finished."

"Nevertheless, I'll be better prepared the next time."

He felt, rather than saw her smile. "There's going to be a next time?"

"Depend on it," he said. "I'm already looking ahead to making love to you here in the moonlight, later on."

"Will you make dinner for me, first?"

He suppressed a twinge of regret at having to deceive her. "Not tonight, princess. I've got a couple of other things I need to take care of. How about I hop over the garden wall and meet you at the top of your grandmother's path around nine? I don't want you navigating it by yourself in the dark. It's too steep."

If she was disappointed, she didn't let it show. "I'll be there," she said.

"And I'll be waiting."

The minute he got back to the house, he phoned Russo. "Is this a good time to talk?"

"Depends on what you have to say," the detective answered.

"I'm interested. If I can help you put Cattanasca away, count me in."

"That's what I was hoping to hear. There's an outdoor café in the piazza behind police headquarters in Positano. Meet me there tomorrow at eleven, but don't sit at the same table. I'll make sure the one next to mine is unoccupied."

"Fine. See you then."

"See you then," Russo repeated. "And remember, Demetrio, not a word to anyone. If mention of what we're planning leaks out, we've lost before we even get started."

"Understood."

The night was balmy. Speckled with stars and dappled in moonlight. Lilies filled the garden with their fragrance as she made her way to the meeting place.

He was already there, a flashlight in his hand, a folded blanket over his arm. "Hey," he said, and hauled her to him for a kiss that sapped her strength to the point that she didn't know how she'd make it down the cliff in one piece.

She needn't have worried. He led the way, stopping often to mark the path with the flashlight beam and guide her safely down until the still-warm sand touched her feet.

He spread the blanket, then asked, "You want to walk a while?"

"If you like."

"I don't," he said. "I'm just trying to show a little restraint."

She slipped the straps of her sundress from her shoulders and let the bodice fall down around her waist. Cupping her breasts, she offered them to him and said, "Please don't. I'm dying for you, Demetrio."

He lowered his head and strung kisses over the slope of each breast. He traced the path of her tan lines with his tongue, and when she was clutching handfuls of his hair, unable to stem the inarticulate little cries of pleasure he induced, he took first one budding nipple in his mouth, then the other, and drew deeply.

She arched her neck, felt the warm, sweet flood of moisture dampen the skin of her inner thighs. Pulling away, she tugged her dress past her hips until it pooled at her feet and showed that she wasn't wearing panties. The devastating need he aroused in her was beyond anything she'd ever expected to know, and it rendered her shameless.

He caught his breath. Touched her fleetingly, sweeping his hand over her mound and dipping one fingertip between the swollen folds of her flesh.

Sensation arrowed the length of her. "Demetrio," she whimpered.

He attacked his own clothing, flinging it aside with utter disregard for where it might land, until he stood as naked as she. "I promised myself I'd pace myself, this time," he whispered, his penis thrusting urgently against her belly. "I intend to hold to that promise."

He eased her down onto the blanket and knelt beside her. Manacled both her hands in one of his and anchored them above her head. Took his mouth on a leisurely journey down her body. Nudged her legs apart.

His tongue flickered like fire at her core, once, twice, and she exploded. And wanted, desperately wanted, to return to him a fraction of the pleasure he inflicted on her. With his head still buried between her thighs, she twisted until she could take him in her mouth.

She swirled her tongue around his smooth, fierce strength and felt him shudder when she closed her lips over his tip. She gloried in her power; in her ability to reduce him to the same blind, mindless delirium he so easily inspired in her. But he showed indomitable resistance and refused to succumb. Instead, as she shattered once again, he moved so that he lay on top of her and finally…finally, he slid inside her.

Their loving this time was slow and deep and gentle. A coming together so sweet, so insistent, that tears rolled down her face at the perfection of it.

To be held and touched and kissed, to be loved by such a man…it wasn't just more than she'd ever hoped to experience, it was more than she thought ever could exist. It was heaven, here on earth. And when the tide rolled over her a third time, tumbling her into ecstasy again, her last coherent thought was to wonder how could she ever have entertained doubts about a man in whom she found such completion of mind, body and soul.

Russo was already there when he arrived at the café, reading the morning paper at one of three small tables in the corner of the piazza. Two middle-aged women chatted over lattes at the second. Demetrio took a seat at the third, his back to Russo, ordered an espresso and leafed through another newspaper left behind by a previous patron.

"Great article in the sports section," Russo commented, turning a page and snapping it into place. "You might want to take it with you when you leave. In the meantime, pretend an interest in the headlines and pay attention."

"Here's the basic plan," the woman sitting closest at the second table remarked conversationally, and proceeded to outline it, while her companion leaned forward, avid-eyed, apparently devouring the latest gossip.

As plans went, it was clean and simple. He was to pretend he'd run out of money and been denied financing from the bank. He was then to approach Cattanasca for help, ask for a sixty-day loan, and agree to put up his property as collateral. He was to play into Cattanasca's hands, agree to his usurious rate of interest, appear to be in over his head for the duration of the loan.

"Sixty days, in other words, which gives us ample time," Russo said, slapping his newspaper down and stretching like a cat, "to gather the evidence we need to put him away. At that point, your work will be done."

"At considerable financial expense to me, it seems."

"No, *signor*," the woman said, with a laugh. "In monetary terms, you will lose nothing. We ask only for your time and cooperation. You will be sold stolen goods, inferior materials and forced to accept the unsafe building services of workers on Cattanasca's payroll. You're an expert in your field. You know what to look for. You are to keep records of every transaction. Inspect and rate the quality of labor performed. We're talking about minute detail, *signor*. Overlook nothing. Think you can handle it?"

Because of Natalie, he'd slept last night for the first time in nearly a week. Because of her, he'd woken that morning, ready to face the day with fresh energy and optimism. If what he'd just learned was the price for having her back in his life, he'd pay it gladly, three times over. "I can handle it. But I don't understand how useful it's going to be."

"You don't have to understand. You're one small but vital cog in a very large wheel, and the less you know about what else is taking place, the easier it will be for you to play your part."

"Don't look now, but our friend Cattanasca's crossing the square and headed this way." Russo rose casually to his feet. "Might be a good idea to check that sports section and retrieve what's hidden there before you become the object of his interest," he said, as he strolled away.

Demetrio found a single sheet of paper slipped between pages one and two, folded it to fit in the inside pocket of his jacket and secreted it there.

"Perfect timing," the woman said. "He's spotted you, *signor*, and is making a beeline for your table. If you're up to it, you can start the ball rolling right away." She rooted in her handbag, brought out a small cosmetics case, looked in the mirror and applied a fresh coat of lipstick. "Are we done here?"

Her companion collected the shopping bags at her feet. "It would seem so," she replied.

Without a single glance in his direction, they left. A minute later, a shadow fell across his newspaper, and he looked up to see Cattanasca depositing an expensive leather briefcase on the table, and taking the seat across from him.

Demetrio rolled up the newspaper and tapped it on the edge of the table.

Let the games begin!

He'd told her, when he'd walked her back to her grand-mother's the night before, that he'd be working all the next day. In what she recognized as a subtle hint that her coming over would interfere with his progress, he'd followed up by saying he'd like to take her out to dinner that evening.

"Out?" she'd echoed in pleased surprise. "As in, a date? In a restaurant?"

"That's pretty much the idea," he said, his smile gleaming in the moonlight. "I can take you someplace where we won't be recognized by your grandmother's friends."

"Oh, I don't care about that." She shook her head, marveling at how quickly life could change from dense black to shining light. Twenty-four hours earlier, it had been all she could do to drum up a smile. Now, she couldn't wipe one off her face. "I just never thought you'd go public about us, that's all, but I'm thrilled to be proved wrong."

"Well, you did tell me your grandmother's gone to Capri, and you know the old saying about what happens when the cat's away."

"The mice will play?"

"Exactly. But flaunting ourselves in her territory is asking for trouble you don't need. I don't want to create unnecessary problems between the pair of you."

"You won't," she said. "I learned years ago how to deal with my grandmother when she goes into control mode. She knows I'm quite capable of moving into a hotel if she tries to interfere with my social life."

"Enough said, then. Pick you up at seven?"

She nodded. "Buzz the intercom, and Romero will activate the gates."

"You think it's a good idea for me to show up at the front door?"

"Demetrio, I've been miserable without you, and I'm done with sneaking around and pretending otherwise. So yes, show up at the front door, unless…will you be driving the truck?"

"Is that a problem?"

"No, but if you like, I can drive. We've got four cars sitting in our garage—"

"I don't like," he said, a hint of chill entering his voice.

"All I'm thinking is that you're spending a fortune fixing your house," she rushed to explain. "Considering the price of gas these days, I don't want to burden you with unnecessary expense on my behalf."

"Let me worry about what I can afford, princess. You just concentrate on having a good time tomorrow night."

She took his advice to heart and spent the day at a spa in Positano, getting the works. Everything from head to toe. Now, with the clock showing ten minutes to seven, all that remained was for her to put on the gauzy cotton dress and step into the high-heeled sandals, both of which she'd bought that morning. A touch of perfume at her pulse points, silver pendant earrings and a garnet dinner ring to complement the dark red roses printed randomly over the pale yellow fabric of her dress, and she was as ready as she'd ever be.

Romero was opening the front door just as she came downstairs, and if he was surprised to find a pickup truck parked under the portico, and her escort for the evening the infamous Demetrio Bertoluzzi, he was too well-trained to let it show.

He helped her into her seat, went around and held open Demetrio's door, and said with great civility, "Enjoy your evening, *signor.*"

"You see?" she said, as the truck rattled down the driveway and through the gates to the road. "That wasn't so difficult, was it?"

He slowed to a stop in the shadow of the estate wall and pulled her across the bench until she was crushed up against him. "Speak for yourself! You look so lovely that, when I saw you, I'd have done then what I'm about to do now, except I was afraid your butler would keel over dead from the shock," he said roughly, and brought his mouth to hers.

The night turned dark as ink, the stars fell away and the moon paled in the heat of his kiss. He cradled her face between his hands. With leisurely finesse, he used his tongue, his lips, his teeth. He stole her breath, he stole her heart. Again. And when he at last drew away, she was trembling all over.

"That'll hold me for now," he said, and turned his attention to negotiating the private road to the highway, with no idea how shaken she was by the emotional intensity he aroused in her.

He took her to Naples, to a little outdoor hole-in-the-wall restaurant on the waterfront in the Bay, where they served wine in colorful ceramic jugs, homemade bread on wooden boards, and pottery bowls of the best cioppino she'd ever tasted.

After the meal, they danced on the uneven paving stones, to a selection of Dean Martin hits picked out on a slightly out-of-tune old piano, by a slightly inebriated old sailor. Natalie was in heaven. The moon shone over the Bay of Naples, fat candles glimmered on the tables, Demetrio held her close, and *Ritorna-Me* had never sounded better.

Before driving home again, they lingered over coffee and grappa, gazed into each other's eyes, and talked about ordinary things, their every word underscored by a simmering subtext that promised another kind of exchange later on.

"What did you do today?" he asked, toying with her fingers.

"Drove into Positano early, and shopped," she said, and thought she must have imagined the wariness that briefly clouded his eyes. "What about you? Did you get everything done that you'd planned?"

"Yeah."

"You spend so much time working on the house, you must be glad to take break for a few hours."

"Uh-huh," he said, and abruptly changed the subject. "When's your grandmother due back?"

"She didn't say. Why?"

He lifted her hand and drew the tip of her middle finger into his mouth. "I'm wondering how much longer I can take advantage of you without her coming after me with a shotgun."

Her smile wobbled alarmingly, partly because it took every ounce of self-restraint not to say: *You can take advantage of me for the rest of your life, if you want to.* And partly because she found his touch, his glance, the timbre of his voice, so unbearably erotic that she almost climaxed, right there and then.

As far as the latter went, he seemed to know. "Shall we get out of here, princess, and go someplace we can be alone?"

"Yes, please," she murmured faintly. "And can we please hurry?"

He took the highway south, but veered off along a quiet road between Castellammare and Sorrento, to where a small, tree-shaded plateau hung out above the water. For a second or two after he killed the engine, they sat like statues, not touching and staring out at the sea, and drinking in the peaceful night. Then, without exchanging a word, they simultaneously reached for one another with the rapacious hunger of lovers reunited after a painful, too-long separation.

He shoved the skirt of her dress up above her knees. Rasped his hand over the skin of her thighs, slid his thumb inside the high-cut leg of her French lace panties. His finger followed. As it delved, stroked, probed, his tongue set fire to her mouth.

She whimpered, melted. Clawed the zipper at his fly. Freed

him and learned the shape of him all over again, tracing the contours of his smooth, hard flesh until he groaned aloud.

He pulled her panties down her legs, flung them onto the dashboard, then moved to her side of the bench, hauled her astride his lap and drove inside her with frenzied desperation.

The old truck rocked and groaned. She braced one hand against the side window, clutched at his shoulder with the other. Opened her eyes and looked into his. Bit her lip and gasped unevenly at the wild, unfettered passion blossoming within her.

The orgasm, striking suddenly and with powerful force, caught her in a vicious, rigid hold and tilted her backward at such an angle that her spine came into contact with the dashboard, and her body touched Demetrio's only where he was buried deep inside her.

She screamed softly at the lavish sensation it caused. He felt it, too, and let loose with a stream of impassioned Italian—rough, explicit descriptions of what she was doing to him, of what he wanted to do to her. She responded by moving against him, a slight thrusting of her hips only. But it was enough.

He tensed. Ground his teeth together until the breath hissed between them. A spasm of exquisite agony crossed his face. He clenched his jaw. A sheen of sweat gleamed faintly on his brow. And, helpless to prevent it, he let his body have its way.

Through half-closed eyes, she watched him come. Felt his scalding explosion run free inside her. Remembered too late that, again, he hadn't used protection. And God help her, she hoped they'd made a baby.

When it was over, he let his head loll against the back of the seat. "That," he panted, "was nothing short of undignified."

"It was real and honest."

CHAPTER TEN

THEY didn't. He drove straight to his place instead, and took her to bed where they made love a second time, then fell asleep in each other's arms, awoke around three, came together again in dreamy pleasure, and then slept again until morning. They'd have lingered there all morning too, until he realized it was nearly nine o'clock and he was late for an appointment in town.

"I'll call you later," he said, and was gone before she had the chance to ask him what was so urgent that he raced off without kissing her goodbye.

She might have known her grandmother would choose to come home late the previous day and, clearly aware Natalie hadn't done likewise, be presiding over the breakfast table in sour solitude. "Do I dare inquire where you've been all night, young woman," she asked, "or shall I simply assume the worst?"

Too euphoric to pretend otherwise, Natalie cooed, "You may assume the worst, as long as you understand that, for me, it was the best."

"You were with him! And here I thought you'd come to your senses."

"As indeed I have," she said, with a beatific smile. "And

you should know that I plan to be with him as often and as long as he'll have me."

A shudder of distaste marred her grandmother's features. "I see."

"I don't think you do."

Barbara sipped her coffee and grimaced as if it tasted like swill. "I can see that you're determined to go to hell in a handbasket, but I don't pretend to understand what it is about this particular man that you find so irresistible."

"Then let me spell it out for you. He's a decent man and he isn't afraid of hard work—something I expect you, of all people, to respect."

"Respecting his work ethic is one thing, Natalie. Rubbing shoulders with him—in a strictly social sense, you understand— quite another. As for how you employed your time together in the night just past..." She shuddered. "I can't begin to imagine."

"Oh, I'm sure you can, if you put your mind to it, Grandmother. Just think back to how you spent the nights with *your* first love. Or have you always put business before pleasure?"

Barbara ignored the question and raised her eyes heavenward, as if seeking divine guidance. "I have absolutely no idea how you could cheapen yourself in such a fashion, with such a man."

"He is a very fine man, and it's time people around here came to realize it."

Her grandmother raised one eyebrow scornfully. "I'm afraid it'll take more than your sleeping with him to make that happen."

"Why? What's his crime? He didn't rape me. He didn't coerce me. I reached the age of consent several years ago, and what I do in private with him is no one's business but his and mine. For the rest, all he wants is to put his grandmother's house in order again. What's wrong with that?"

"In and of itself, nothing. If anything, we're glad he's

doing something about that disgracefully run-down house. But none of that changes the fact that he doesn't fit in here and he never will, because he's simply not our sort."

"Well, he's *my* sort, so you'd better get used to it! He knows what he wants, and he's not afraid to go after it. He's well aware what you all think of him, but he's focused on achieving his own goals, not catering to yours. Impressing people isn't on his agenda."

"Yet he appears to have impressed you, my darling."

"Because he's a real man," she shot back, a flush warming her face. "And quite frankly, I haven't come across too many of them lately."

Observing her narrowly, her grandmother said, "Well, I'll grant him this. He's made more of an impact on you in a few weeks than Lewis Madison did in years. I don't recall your ever defending *him* so passionately. Mind you, Lewis probably never did anything that required defending in the first place."

"Oh, really, Grandmother!" Natalie slumped in weary disgust. "Why can't you cut Demetrio a break?"

"And exactly why should I do that?"

"Because he deserves better than to be treated like an outcast around here, just because he doesn't drive a fancy car or belong to the right clubs. All it would take is one word from you to change that attitude."

"You give me too much credit, my dear."

"No. People look up to you. They follow where you lead."

"What are you getting at, Natalie?" her grandmother said sharply.

"I want you to give a dinner party, and invite him."

"Him—and other people?"

"Yes!" she snapped. "What did you think I meant, him and his dog?"

"He wouldn't accept!"

"He might, especially if I encouraged him to. And if he did, it could mark the beginning of a new era for him."

Her grandmother regarded her pityingly. "Are you seriously so besotted with the man that you don't see how absurd you're being? He'd be hopelessly out of his depth. If I were to agree to invite him here for dinner, all you'd succeed in doing is embarrass him dreadfully." She shook her head. "Natalie, my darling, saying 'no' to you isn't easy, but in this instance, I'm afraid I must."

"You're being unfair! He deserves a chance to prove himself."

"Then let him do it at someone else's table, because he's not doing it at mine. Not even for you will I subject my friends to an evening of that man's company. I'm sorry, Natalie, but that's my final word on the subject."

For over a month, it was the final word on any subject of import between Natalie and her grandmother. Although they maintained a civil enough relationship, the prevailing atmosphere in the Villa Rosamunda remained cool, to say the least.

Not so, though, at the house next door. Sometimes, Natalie would spend several consecutive days there, weeding the flower beds, planting rosemary and tarragon and oregano and basil in the herb garden, and generally weaving her way into the fabric of Demetrio's life.

She prepared simple lunches of bread and olives and cheese and fresh figs, which they ate on the back patio. She leash-trained Pippo and taught him basic obedience, and brushed his coat until it gleamed like thick black satin.

Often, Demetrio fixed dinner for them, and she'd stay the night. They'd make love, and bathe together in the big, claw-footed, cast-iron tub, and sip coffee in bed in the mornings, and do all the things married people do. And she'd nurse the hope that, one day, he might propose, and instead of playing at being a couple, they'd really become one, in the eyes of the church, the law and society in general.

But every Eden had its serpent, and theirs was no exception. Sometimes, for no apparent reason, he'd send her home and tell her to wait until he called before she came back again. "Too much going on around here," he'd say. Or, "You'll just be underfoot and could get hurt."

Well, there was certainly plenty going on because, all of a sudden, he seemed to have enough money that he could bring in all sorts of extra help. Horrid, sleazy-looking individuals, who made more mess than they started with, and who, if she happened to be there, would watch her out of the corners of their eyes and snigger among themselves. But when she questioned him about them, Demetrio cut her off abruptly and withdrew into a brooding silence.

One time, when he was outside talking to them about something, the newly installed house phone rang. Not wanting him to miss a possibly important call, she went to answer, but had barely lifted the handset before he raced into the kitchen and grabbed it out her hand.

"I'll call you right back," he practically barked into the mouthpiece, and hung up. Then, turning to her, he said in a voice that made her blood run cold, "Don't ever answer my phone again."

Stunned, she backed away from him. "I was just trying to help, Demetrio."

"Stop trying. I don't need your help," he snapped, and went back outside. Peeping through the window, she saw him pacing up and down the pool deck, his cell phone to his ear, his expression stony.

The way he shut her out both hurt and frightened her. Why couldn't he trust her? What was he hiding? And why was she tolerating such bad behavior?

Annoyed at her own weakness, she collected her things and left the house, but didn't get halfway down the driveway before he caught up with her and pulled her into his arms. "Don't go," he whispered against her mouth, peppering his words with tiny, frantic kisses. "I'm sorry! I had no right speaking to you that way."

She kissed him back and buried her doubts. Except they wouldn't stay buried because, although he never did speak to her like that again, he was often moody, preoccupied, secretive.

Then, one day, he announced he had to drive to Naples for some hardware he'd ordered to go with the custom-built kitchen cabinets that were to be installed the following week. When she offered to go with him, he asked her to stay and keep Pippo company, but said he'd bring home one of the thick-crust pizzas for which Naples was famous.

"We'll dine al fresco by the pool, with a bottle of local wine, then go skinny-dipping," he promised.

That evening was touched with the kind of magic that had made so many evenings with him unforgettable, but sadly was becoming increasingly absent. Yet for all that he played the role of romantic lover, he didn't ask her to stay overnight, and the niggling doubts she tried so hard to suppress clamored more urgently than ever to be acknowledged.

Something was wrong. She felt it in her bones. And whatever it was, he was going to extraordinary lengths to try to hide it from her.

The next morning, for the first time in weeks, she made a point of joining her grandmother for breakfast. "It's nice to have you sitting across the table from me again," Barbara said, and the tender affection in her words was all it took for Natalie to burst into tears.

Misunderstanding the reason, her grandmother said, "Oh,

darling, I've been miserable, as well! I hate it when we're on the outs with each other."

"Me, too," she sobbed into her linen serviette.

"Well, at least things are progressing next door. I see Mr. Bertoluzzi is erecting a new wall along the front of his property."

Wrestling her emotions under control, she said, "I'm happy just knowing a new kitchen's going in next week. The old one's a disgrace."

"You don't *sound* happy, Natalie," her grandmother observed gently. "You don't *look* very happy, either. Are things not going well between the two of you?"

There was nothing snide or satisfied in the question, and suddenly Natalie wanted to confide in the one woman she knew would always be on her side, no matter what. "Most of the time they are. But I don't always understand him as well as I might."

Her grandmother regarded her a moment, started to speak, then seemed to think better of it and snapped her mouth closed again.

"If you've got something on your mind, Grandmother," she said wearily, "you might as well air it."

Barbara lifted her shoulders in a shrug. "Perhaps the real problem has less to do with understanding him, than it has with the fact that you don't know him as well as you think you do."

"Don't talk in riddles. I'm not up to dealing with them. Just say what you have to say."

"Very well. Marianna Sorrentino mentioned that she saw him yesterday."

"I'm not surprised. He had to go to Naples."

"Not in Naples, darling. In Positano, at a sidewalk coffee shop, in the middle of the morning—and in the company of a very undesirable character with a most unsavory reputation. You wouldn't know this man, of course, and I can promise you, he's not someone you'd *want* to know."

"Because you classify him as being too much lik Demetrio?"

"Dear heaven, I hope not! This person is much, muc worse. He is, in a word, despicable. In fact, I recall mention ing him to you briefly when you first arrived and asked hov the Bertoluzzis ever managed to move into the neighborhood.

Natalie's heart plummeted and she wanted nothing mor than to clap her hands over her ears and refuse to listen t anything further. But the demon within would stand for non of that. "What's this man's name?"

"Guido Cattanasca—not that that will mean anything to you.

The blood drained to her ankles, leaving her light-headec and she was afraid she was going to lose the little breakfas she'd managed to consume.

"Natalie?" Her grandmother's voice floated from a vas distance. "Are you all right?"

"No," she whispered, staggering to her feet. "I must hav eaten something that disagrees with me."

She made it to her bathroom just in time. And wished sh could attribute her vomiting to shock. But the truth was, thi was the third morning in a row that she'd thrown up. She tol herself it was just stress, but was terribly afraid her prayers that night in the truck, on the quiet little plateau overlookin the sea, had been answered.

Be careful what you wish for! wise people always said. Bu she'd heeded the warning too late and might very well b carrying the child of someone who, contrary to what she des perately wished she could believe, seemed less the man sh wanted him to be, and more the man he was feared to be.

She was left with only one option, of course, and that wa to confront him. So even though he'd asked her to stay hom that day, as soon as her stomach settled, she marched righ over to his place.

The high stucco wall running along the front of his property was almost finished, and two men were busy installing tall, wrought-iron gates at the foot of the driveway. Before long, Demetrio wouldn't need to issue orders when he didn't want her around. All he'd have to do was lock the gates to keep her out.

She found him in the day salon, consulting with the man in charge of the painting crew he'd hired. Before her courage deserted her, she interrupted them with a curt, "I need to speak to you, Demetrio. Right now."

At her tone, his long black lashes flared in surprise around his too-beautiful blue eyes. "Okay. Give me a minute and I'll meet you on the terrace."

It was cool out there in the shade. Cool and deceptively peaceful—to a stranger's eye, at least. But it wasn't enough to shake her sense that something evil was at work below the surface.

Behind her, the French doors swished open and Demetrio stepped out. He came up behind her, dropped a kiss on the back of her neck and spanned her waist with his hands. "You seem upset, princess, what's wrong?"

She pulled away and turned slowly to face him, dreading what she had to ask. "Where did you really go, yesterday, and who did you see?"

"What do you mean, *really go?* You know where I went. To Naples to pick up the hardware for the new kitchen cabinets. You saw me bring it into the house when I got home."

"Where else, besides Naples?"

He frowned, and his face took on the closed expression she'd come to dread. "What's with the third degree, Natalie?"

"I don't consider that an answer to my question."

"I don't consider you have the right to quiz me as if you're my mother, and I'm a teenager who broke curfew."

She held his gaze. "Exactly *what* am I to you, Demetrio?"

Exasperated, he slapped a hand to his forehead. "For Pete's sake, woman, I'm up to my neck in problems enough. Can't this wait for another time?"

"No," she said. "I want to know now, before matters go any further."

"Matters?" he exploded. "What *matters?*"

"Us, Demetrio!" she cried. "Who we are and what we mean to each other."

"I'd have thought that was obvious."

"I'd have thought so, too, until you gave me reasons to doubt you."

"And exactly how have I done that?"

"You've lied to me," she said baldly. "More than once, I might add."

He flushed a dark red and his eyes sparked fire. "If you were a man, I'd deck you for saying that."

"And I'd give everything I have to hear you say I'm mistaken."

"I shouldn't have to tell you that," he said quietly. "You ought to know me well enough to trust me. Why do you find that so difficult, Natalie? Because I'm a Bertoluzzi?"

"No," she said, her voice breaking. "Because I love you and I want to believe in you, but you're making that impossible. And because you were seen having coffee in Positano, when you were supposed to be in Naples buying hardware."

His jaw tightened ominously. "Seen by whom?"

"It doesn't matter. It's enough that I heard about it from someone other than you."

"Since when is it such a big deal for a man to stop for coffee in one town, when he's on his way home from another?"

"Since he chooses to do it in the company of a man called Cattanasca."

He turned pale beneath his tan. Lowered his lashes to half-mast. Shook his head. "Oh, princess!"

"Is it true?"

"Yes," he said, looking her straight in the eye again. "It's true."

"You told me you wanted nothing to do with him, but you sit down and have coffee with him? Add another lie to the list, Demetrio!"

He cursed under his breath, an ugly gutter obscenity, and glared at her. Then, moving so suddenly that she had no time to evade him, he stepped toward her with his hand raised and swung it at her head.

"Keep still," he growled as he did it. "A spider—"

But for the first time ever, she was actually afraid of him, and had already flinched and ducked aside. Worse yet, there was no disguising her reaction.

"What the devil…?" Thunderstruck, he stopped in midswing. "You thought I was going to *hit* you?"

"No," she whispered, heart battering against her ribs. "No, I didn't. Really, I didn't!"

He let his hand fall limply to his side and shook his head again. "Yes, you did," he said in hollow disbelief. "Who's lying now, Natalie?"

The look on his face undid her. She saw the pain in his eyes. She saw his stunning male beauty—the thick dark hair, the eyes that pierced straight to her soul, the mouth that could make her want so badly that she cried—and knew in that moment that she loved him and that, by itself, love wasn't enough.

Overcome with a terrible sense of loss, she sighed and said, "I'm sorry if that's—"

"Save it!" he said, with tightly leashed, steely control. "I have hit men, and I'd do it again without a moment's hesitation if it meant defending a helpless creature. But I have never struck a woman in my life, and I don't propose to start now, with you. Why do you find that so difficult to believe, Natalie? Why assume the worst? Why can't you just trust me to do what I think is best?"

"I trust you."

But the quiver in her voice betrayed her doubts. "How much?" he asked harshly.

"About as much you trust me." The tears rolled down her face. "And it seems that's not nearly enough, is it?"

"Son of a bitch!" As though to rein in his anger before it got the better of him, he strode rapidly up and down the terrace several times before confronting her again and, sounding marginally less agitated, said, "This is insane. You realize that, don't you? I'm sorry you found out about Cattanasca, but there's a perfectly reasonable explanation for my being seen with him, and I'd have told you about it myself except that he's not worth wasting time over.

"He stopped by my table to repeat his offer to buy this house, and I turned him down again. That's it. But if my keeping this from you has turned you against me to the point that you want to end things between us, just say the word and I'll stay out of your life. If not, then let's get together later on and try to sort out where we stand."

"I don't want to end things," she said.

His touch gentle, he cupped her face in both his hands. "Neither do I, princess," he said softly. "Neither do I."

The French doors swung open again. "We need you in here, Bertoluzzi," a coarse-looking man in orange overalls shouted. "You're holding things up."

"I've got to get back to work," he murmured, pinning her in his gaze. "And you look wiped out. Go home and get some rest. I'll finish up early here and pick you up around two. We'll drive to Positano, take the hydrofoil to Capri, spend the rest of the afternoon there, then come back to the mainland and have dinner in Ravello."

The tenderness in his voice, in his eyes, melted her reservations and gave her new hope that they could still make the relationship work. "That sounds wonderful."

"Then it's a date. I'll see you at two."

He watched her leave, his emotions in turmoil.

She was right to doubt him. Since joining forces with Russo and his cohorts, he'd lied to her over and over again. Until the whole nasty business with Cattanasca was over, he had no choice but to continue doing so, not just because he was sworn to secrecy, but because he'd go to any lengths to shield her from the stink of corruption that was Cattanasca's most distinctive feature.

The man made his skin crawl. Had done so from that first fortuitous meeting at the sidewalk café.

"You look down in the mouth, my young friend," he'd said, oozing sympathy so phony, a blind man could have seen it a mile away.

Playing the part assigned to him, Demetrio had assumed an air of abject misery. "You would, too, if you were down to your last hundred euros and no bank wanted to give you the time of day."

"So money's the problem, eh?" Cattanasca sighed and placed his liver-spotted hand on his arm. It had been all Demetrio could do not to smack it aside. "Isn't it always the case? But it just so happens I can help you, just as I've helped others in your position. How much money are we talking about?"

It had cost him dearly to reply with fawning, nauseating humility, "Thousands, *signor*. Because you were right. It's costing me more than I ever dreamed to restore my home, and I'm tapped out."

"Thousands are not a problem for me, my boy, and I'm reasonable man. I'm sure we can reach an agreement. How does this sound?"

The terms he'd rattled off, with the interest doubling after thirty days, and tripling after sixty, were extortion pure and simple. "And then, of course, there's the little matter of security," he finished. "You understand, I'm sure, that you'll need to put up some sort of collateral."

"How about my truck?"

"How about your villa?"

You asshole! How many poor saps have you gouged, and left with nothing? How many have you driven to suicide? "I can't risk losing the villa."

"You've already done that, Demetrio," Cattanasca informed him. "What do you think is going to happen to it when your creditors come calling?"

Almost gagging with the effort, he'd looked suitably forlorn. "You've got a point."

And if I could lay hands on something sharp enough, I'd drive it through your avaricious heart!

"Don't let it get you down," Cattanasca crowed, waving to attract the waiter's attention and ordering two espressos. "It's not the end of the world. I'll do more than lend you money, my friend. I'll put you in touch with people who'll cut you a deal on supplies and labor. It'll all work out in the end, you'll see."

Sure it will—hugely in your favor!

More resolved than ever to beat the bastard at his own game, Demetrio had signed the printed agreement Cattanasca just happened to carry in his briefcase. "If I didn't know better, I'd think you came here prepared," he said, shoving the sheet of paper back across the table.

"I'm always prepared to step in when a man needs a helping

hand," Cattanasca smirked. "I'll be in touch every few days, to see how you're doing. I like to keep track of my investments."

He'd phoned several times since, to arrange face-to-face meetings Demetrio would dearly have liked to avoid. But his job was to collect any information he was able to glean and pass it on to Russo and his associates. He still didn't know if what he gave them proved useful, and he didn't care. He just wanted the job over and done with, and to that end, did his best to expedite matters.

For his own peace of mind, he always made sure to reserve two days every week when he could rid himself of the fly-by-night tradesmen Cattanasca steered his way, and be free to repair their shoddy workmanship with the top-grade materials he had hidden in his garage. On those same days, he made up some excuse to keep Natalie away, too, because there was no way he could explain such seemingly irrational behavior on his part.

But it all took a toll. He felt he was dancing on the thin edge of a very sharp blade. The illicit meetings, the lowlifes crawling over his property, the seediness of the whole operation in which he was taking part smacked too much of his grandfather's era, and he was finding it increasingly difficult to hide his disgust.

Not a good thing, he knew. Sometimes the look in Cattanasca's reptilian eyes gave him pause. The man was no fool and he'd make a very bad enemy.

On the positive side, he had only a couple more days left before his role in the sting came to an end and Cattanasca would cease to be a threat. As far as Demetrio was concerned, it couldn't happen soon enough.

The French doors banged open again. "Hey, Bertoluzzi!" the same roughneck bellowed. "Are you planning to tell us what you want us to do in here, or should we just pack it in and go home?"

"Go home," he said, his appetite for intrigue suddenly exhausted. "In fact, take your stuff and don't bother to come back."

CHAPTER ELEVEN

THE afternoon in Capri marked a turning point in their relationship that made Natalie glad she'd been brave enough to confront Demetrio.

"I'm making some changes," he told her. "I'm beginning to realize I've taken on too much with the renovation, and I'm bringing in better qualified people to help me finish the job—an out-of-town company with a reputation for top-notch work. And before you ask, I have a couple of savings bonds I can cash in, to cover my costs."

A few days later, two big vans and a truck painted a rich, metallic green, rolled up his driveway, *Emerenzia Costruzione* inscribed in subdued gold on their doors. The team of men who arrived with them took over the completion of the work with professional expertise. Almost immediately, Demetrio lost the edge of irritability, the bursts of sudden, inexplicable temper that had defined his behavior in recent weeks, and became again the man she'd first fallen in love with.

It probably helped that she herself was more relaxed when she realized she wasn't pregnant, after all. She wanted children someday, and she wanted Demetrio to be their father, but bringing a baby into the mix at this stage would have been fair to no one, and the reason for that was simple. Things between her and Demetrio might be better, but they still weren't perfect.

For a start, he asked her to stay home when the new crew was at work, and although she understood that her being in the way would slow down progress and end up costing him more, she wished he'd at least let her drop by to visit Pippo once in a while. But he was adamant. "Company regulations. No women in a hard-hat area," he told her. "And at this point, there isn't a room in the house or a place in the garden that isn't a hard-hat area."

On the other hand, he encouraged her to spend as many evenings with him as she could spare. To stay overnight if she wished, as long as she was gone before the working day began. On those occasions, he was tender, he was passionate, he was considerate. He told her she was beautiful, desirable and that he missed her when she wasn't with him.

But he never once said he loved her. He never made reference to a time beyond the immediate future. He uttered not a single promise. Instead he gave her the gift of passionate, unforgettable nights which she hoarded as if they were matchless pearls suspended on a very frail string.

Stir them up all you like, but oil and water aren't meant to mix, princess, he'd warned her, more than once, and the words came back to haunt her in the early morning hours when she lay at his side and watched him sleep, with the moon playing shadows over his face and shrouding it in secrets.

That Barbara recognized all was not smooth sailing in Natalie's life, and was worried about her, was hard to miss. Barbara *hovered*—and she wasn't the hovering type. She waded into the fray and wrestled life into submission when it didn't go her way. Knowing that as well as she did, Natalie shouldn't have been surprised to learn that her grandmother had taken action.

"I found this in my mailbox this morning," Demetrio said one evening, showing her an embossed vellum envelope.

She recognized the crest in the top left hand corner and the handwriting scrawled across the front, and a tremor of foreboding fluttered over her. "What is it?"

"An invitation to dinner at your grandmother's, this coming Saturday. What do you suppose that's all about?"

She hoped she managed to contain her dismay as she struggled to come up with an explanation. "Well, it's clear enough, surely? She wants you to come to dinner."

"Did you know about it beforehand?"

"In a way. We sort of discussed the idea, a few weeks ago. But then, as you know, she and I had a bit of a falling-out, and the subject never came up again. I assumed she'd forgotten about it."

He tapped the envelope against the palm of his hand. "I wonder why she resurrected it?"

"I suppose," she ventured haltingly, "because she thinks it's time you met your neighbors."

"It's a bit late in the day for that, wouldn't you say? I've had neighbors since the day I came back here, but this is the first time one of them has felt moved to throw a welcome home party for me."

"Well, she's more than just one of your neighbors, Demetrio. She's my grandmother and she knows we're..." An item? A couple? Lovers? "Seeing one another. Perhaps giving us her public seal of approval is all this is about."

He laughed out loud at that. "Sweetheart, I admire your belief in the good intentions of others, but I'd bet money your grandmother wishes I'd drop off the edge of the earth, and in some ways I can hardly blame her. If it were *my* daughter fooling around with a man like me, I'd take a shotgun to him."

Well, that certainly answered her question. They were neither a couple, nor an item. They were simply "fooling around!" "If attending makes you uncomfortable, you can always send your regrets."

He resorted to his familiar sideways glance and secretive little smile. "And show myself a coward, afraid to face her? Not a chance! I'll be there, as, I presume, will you."

"Naturally," she said, even though there was nothing at all natural in the sudden turn of events.

By the time Saturday night rolled around, she was a bundle of nerves, her every instinct on high alert. Not so very long ago, she'd have embraced her grandmother's change of heart on the subject of asking Demetrio to dinner. Now, it left her sick to her stomach because, with every passing hour since she'd learned of the impending dinner party, she'd grown more convinced than ever that her grandmother's motives for hosting it were far from pure.

Not that Barbara admitted as much. "I don't know why you're taking this attitude," she said, when Natalie tackled her on the subject. "You're the one who brought up the idea in the first place."

"And you're the one who refused to entertain it."

"Since when am I not allowed to change my mind? I can see that you're devoted to the man. I thought you'd be pleased."

"Not when you go behind my back, Grandmother. You should have discussed this with me before you went ahead with the invitation."

"I wanted to surprise you, darling, and I'm sorry if it backfired, but there's not much I can do about that now. Everyone's accepted, including your Mr. Bertoluzzi, so I'm afraid you'll just have to get over your little hissy fit and make up your mind to enjoy the evening."

Enjoy? Fat chance! Positioned near the terrace doors to give herself a clear view of the entire room, Natalie fixed yet another smile on a face already aching from the effort of appearing happy and relaxed, and tried to respond appropriately to the conversation swirling around her, all the time keeping her eyes trained on the foyer beyond the salon. Although everyone else had arrived, of Demetrio there was still no sign, and part of her hoped he'd changed his mind and decided to stay home.

Earlier, though, he'd sent a gorgeous flower arrangement to her grandmother, and even *she'd* had to admit it was the mark of a man with enough social know-how not to burden his hostess with last-minute tokens of appreciation when she was busy entertaining a roomful of guests. It was hardly the gesture of a man not planning to show up for the main event.

More agitated by the minute, Natalie sneaked a glance at the gilt clock on the mantelpiece. She'd taken hours to get ready, unable to decide between an exquisite designer cocktail dress and a simpler outfit, just in case Demetrio either didn't realize it was a black-tie evening, or didn't own a dinner suit.

In the end, looking her best for him had won out. She'd chosen the designer number, a peacock-blue beaded affair, with high-heeled peau de soie pumps dyed to match. She'd coiled her hair in a smooth knot on the crown of her head, applied a shimmer of eye shadow, stroked mascara over her lashes and tucked a tiny bosom bag scented with her favorite fragrance inside her bra. But much more of this hanging around waiting for the ax to fall, and she'd change into shorts and a top, scrub the makeup off her face, then run over to the Villa Delfina, tell Demetrio the party was canceled and settle in for the kind of evening that carried no hidden agenda.

And then, Demetrio finally showed up. If there'd been an ounce of justice in the world, his arrival would have gone unnoticed, and he'd have melted inconspicuously into the crowd. But that was not to be. The very second Romero opened the front door to admit him, an uncanny electricity seemed to shoot through the atmosphere, leaving everyone temporarily paralyzed.

Trays of canapés in hand, the extra help hired for the evening froze in place. The buzz of conversation sank into thudding silence as the assembled guests, the Pol Roger in their Venetian champagne flutes forgotten, eyed him with astounded amusement.

One would have thought an alien had descended into their midst, and that might just as well have been the case. It wasn't the fact that he was the only man present not attired in traditional black tie that sent eyebrows shooting to the ceiling, so much as what he'd chosen to wear in its place.

In all fairness, he *had* selected a black-on-black striped tie, but he'd teamed it with a black pin-striped suit and a charcoal-gray shirt. That he was flawlessly attired right down to his highly polished black leather shoes counted for nothing. His monochromatic choice of clothing simply struck too sinister a note, and he himself exuded too much raw masculinity for that refined gathering.

Natalie knew it, even before a woman close by murmured none too discreetly to her husband, "Dear God, the Mafia has joined the party! What *was* Barbara thinking of to invite him?"

Natalie's heart lurched sickeningly. She wanted to hustle him out of the line of fire. Defy anyone to level another unkind word his way. Berate him for showing so little common sense. Most of all, she wanted to hurl invectives at her grandmother for choreographing a situation deliberately designed to humiliate him and embarrass her.

The time for action, however, had been when she'd first

learned of the dinner party. If she'd dissuaded him then from attending, he would not now be the focus of such malicious attention. But she'd left it too late and could do nothing but stand rooted to the floor, beseeching him with her eyes to forgive her for not having suspected all along that he was walking into a setup.

Surprisingly unfazed at finding himself the object of such prolonged and brutal scrutiny, Demetrio surveyed the room at large and inclined his head at her grandmother, the only person present beside himself still apparently in command of her faculties.

Approaching him, she cooed with thinly veiled disdain, "Well, Mr. Bertoluzzi, here you are at last! I was beginning to think you weren't going to put in an appearance."

That his response took her by complete surprise was obvious from the startled expression that flitted across her face when, instead of shaking her proffered hand, he raised the back of it briefly to his lips, and purred in that sexy accented way he did so well, "I wouldn't dream of reneging on so charming a hostess, *signora*. It is my very great pleasure to be here."

Then, looking her straight in the eye, he winked.

He might just as well have come right out and said, *We both know we're lying, but if that's how you want to play this out, it's fine by me.*

"Well... Good gracious, where are my manners?" Whether a blush stained her grandmother's cheeks might be have been open to question, but there was no doubt she was more flustered than Natalie had ever seen her. "Let's find you a glass of champagne, and I'll introduce you to everyone."

"Champagne sounds like a fine idea," he replied, his voice lilting with amusement, "but I rather doubt introductions are necessary. I'm sure your guests know very well who I am."

Natalie feared her grandmother was about to choke at that. Recovering Barbara protested, "But *you* aren't familiar with *them*, Mr. Bertoluzzi."

This time, he favored her with a full-blown smile. "I'm familiar with your granddaughter, though."

"So you are." She subjected him to one of her razor-sharp stares. "You and she have become quite close, I understand."

He didn't flinch. "Quite," he agreed. "About as close as a man and a woman can get, in fact."

A faint gasp rippled over the room. They ignored it, and for a moment, their gazes locked in combat. But just as Natalie could never dwell too long on those heavily lashed, piercing blue eyes without losing her composure, neither, it seemed, could her grandmother.

"Well, then," she practically wheezed, stepping out of the line of fire before her dignity was reduced to shreds, and beckoning to Natalie, "I'll leave you in her capable hands. Hopefully she'll succeed where I have failed, and can persuade you to widen your circle of acquaintances."

At last freed from the paralyzing spell he'd cast on the room, Natalie joined them. "Hi," she murmured, so acutely aware that the spotlight had been turned on her that she didn't know if she should drum up another strained smile and pretend all was well, or simply fall into his arms and burst into tears.

He solved her dilemma by squeezing her hands, kissing her on both cheeks, then stepping back and saying, "I've never seen you more beautiful, princess."

Who was this man, so adept at saying just the right thing? she asked herself, momentarily struck speechless by his savoir faire.

She wasn't the only one wondering. When he'd first arrived, it was if the bubonic plague had blown into the room, but the balance of power had shifted since then. He'd emerged the winner in a subtle battle of wills with the formidable Barbara Wade, and those who'd have turned their backs on him a few minutes before, regarded him now with grudging respect. Black tie or not, their glances said, he merited a second look.

She had to agree. He'd tamed his often-unruly hair into sleek submission and erased every hint of five-o'clock shadow. His fingernails were clipped short and scrupulously clean; his aftershave lotion discreet and tasteful. And while his choice of apparel could hardly be considered conservative, there was no denying the tailored excellence of his suit, or the fine quality of his silk shirt and tie. Natalie had little doubt, as she made the rounds with him, that he could handle himself with a whole lot more dazzle and aplomb than she was able to command.

He didn't disappoint, acknowledging each introduction with understated courtesy and a sophistication she both admired and resented. Who was he really fooling here—her, or everyone else?

She suspected she wasn't the only one left wondering. Although the men shook his hand, and the women responded with guarded smiles, when the dinner gong sounded and they all trooped to the dining room, Natalie sensed they still expected he'd commit some horrendous faux pas and could hardly wait to see him cut down to size.

He failed to accommodate them, dispensing easy charm on the women seated on either side of him and bending his head attentively to listen to their remarks. He knew exactly which fork to use, which glass to raise, and displayed a comprehensive knowledge of international politics, finance and sports.

Finally a woman farther down the table couldn't stand it a minute longer, and asked, "How do you come to be so extraordinarily well-informed on such diverse topics, Mr. Bertoluzzi?"

At any other time, Natalie would have found the question gauche and distinctly offensive. Just then, she could hardly wait to hear his reply.

"I spent several years traveling the world, *signora*."

"Oh, really?" the woman drawled. "Do tell us where."

He shrugged his impressive shoulders and bathed her in a confiding smile. "A few months in Asia, Australia and the Middle East, but mostly in the United States."

Regarding him with almost lascivious fascination, she took a hasty gulp of her wine. "And where in the United States, exactly?"

"Mainly New Jersey."

The tidbit of information, casually dropped, caused a stir of interest that wasn't kind. People smiled behind their hands and exchanged smug glances, their immediate assumption appearing to be that he must have been involved in the seamy side of life unfortunately associated with certain areas of the Garden State—until, with stellar timing, he added lazily, "At Princeton."

A smattering of astonished laughter erupted. "You surely can't be referring to the Ivy League university?" someone else inquired.

"I surely can," he replied blandly.

"What on earth did you do there?"

"Played poker and basketball…" Again, his timing was impeccable. "When I wasn't attending classes, that is."

"Attending classes?" This time, Barbara posed the question. "You were a student at Princeton, Mr. Bertoluzzi?"

"Why, yes, Signora Wade," he said, further taking the wind out of her sails, as well as everyone else's. "How else could I lay claim to a graduate degree in economics?"

"How else, indeed!" Recovering, Barbara eyed him appraisingly a moment, then lifted her glass in a rueful toast. "My, my, Mr. Bertoluzzi, it would seem I have woefully underestimated you."

Again, he favored her with his dazzling smile. "Don't beat yourself up over it, *signora*," he said. "Most people do, on first acquaintance."

Natalie wasn't nearly as impressed. All the doubts she thought she'd buried, all the little inconsistencies she'd tried to justify, surged to new life. While a babble of comments and questions swirled around her, the only voice she heard was the one in her head.

Who is this man, and what ever made you think you knew him? it asked. *How many more surprises does he hold in store, and when is he going to reveal them?*

He slept late on the Sunday, waking just after nine. Stretched on the deep, new, comfortable mattress on his big, new, comfortable bed, and folded his hands behind his head. Across the room, the glass doors to the loggia stood open, commanding a stunning view across the Tyrrhenian Sea, all the way to distant Sicily.

Fitting that this had been his first night in the master suite, he thought, filled with rare elation. It made vindication that much sweeter. He'd overcome the odds before, more times than he cared to count, but none compared to what he'd accomplished last night.

It had started with Russo's unexpected visit, and the news that the undercover police operation had come to a successful close. The young detective had been willing, eager even, to explain how, but Demetrio hadn't wanted to know. It was enough that he'd played a small part in the outcome.

It had ended with Barbara Wade's dinner party. Not that

he fooled himself into believing that one night was all it would take for him to be accepted into that fold of old-money aristocrats gathered around her elegant table, but then, nor had he ever expected to be.

What mattered was that he'd emerged the uncontested winner in a skirmish intended to put him to rout and thereby rid the neighborhood of a blight it had been forced to tolerate for far too long—and which ended with them scratching their heads and questioning how he'd managed to beat them at their own game.

He could have told them how, but he was prepared to offer explanations only to Natalie because, from the outset, she'd embraced him exactly as he appeared to be and never once asked him to change.

She'd seen past his pride, and loved him for the man he was inside. Because of her unconditional acceptance, he'd finally been able to shed the bitterness which had dogged him for so long, and realized only when he'd let it go, how heavy a burden he'd carried all these years.

Closing his eyes, he smiled, free at last to acknowledge the yearnings she aroused in him. Of marrying, and starting a family. Of children who, untainted by the past, would never know the hurt of rejection or shame. Children who'd grow up proud to carry the name Bertoluzzi.

If she accepted his proposal, then the endless, back-breaking work, the labor of love involved in restoring the villa, achieved a purpose that went far beyond raising a monument to the memory of his grandmother. It became his gift to the woman he knew he'd love long past death and into eternity; his legacy to the children she'd bear him.

The bedside phone rang. Still smiling, eyes still closed, he reached over and brought the handset to his ear. *"Ciao."*

"It's Natalie," he heard her say. "And we need to talk."

CHAPTER TWELVE

HE WAS outside when she arrived, standing next to his old truck and talking to two of the men he'd hired to replace the former crew. "I won't be long," he said, motioning her inside the house.

She didn't mind the wait. It gave her the opportunity to look around. The changes that had taken place since the new workmen had taken over boggled the mind.

Polished marble, gleaming floors, plaster cornices and wooden moldings, all restored to their former glory, met the eye at every turn. The scent of beeswax and lemon oil hung in the air. Furniture was in place, most of it new, but with a few lovely antique pieces belonging to his grandmother, which he'd put in storage at the time of her death.

A Murano glass vase in shades of purple and ruby showed itself off to perfection in a wall niche painted white. Another piece of Murano, this time a leaping dolphin, shimmering in the sunlight streaming down the stairs from the window on the first landing, sat on a black marble pedestal in front of the cascading drama of an eight-foot-tall bronze water wall.

Except for an intricately carved ebony grand piano and strategically placed pots of greenery, the main salon was all sleek oyster-white leather upholstery, alabaster lamps and glass occasional tables. Airy and spacious, it drew the eye to

the terrace beyond the open French doors, and at this time o
year appeared more an extension of the garden than part o
the house itself. Yet she could imagine how it would appea
in December, with blazing logs in the white marble fireplace
and dark red poinsettias gracing the hearth and tabletops.

Who *was* the owner of this tastefully restored villa set ir
manicured grounds, and where had he found the money to create
it? Or perhaps more pertinently, *what* was he? Lover or liar?

"Talk?" he'd purred suggestively, when she'd phoned. "
can think of better ways to spend the day. How are you thi:
morning, my darling?"

Oh, a fine time to start handing out the endearments!

She'd steeled herself to remain strong and resolute, ever
though both her brain and her legs threatened to turn to mush
"Decidedly confused," she'd replied, recalling her grandmother's comments as they sipped their mimosas before
brunch.

"That young man took us all by surprise, darling—excep
for you, of course. Naturally, you already knew there wa:
more to him than met the eye."

Naturally—not!

She'd barely slept as she struggled to understand why he'c
kept so much about himself secret, but had arrived at no sat-
isfactory conclusions. In fact, his behavior had brought all her
previous doubts in glaring focus. However he might try to ra-
tionalize his actions, as far as she was concerned they addec
up to nothing short of unforgivable duplicity.

The old truck's door slammed. Its engine sputtered to life
followed by the sound of its tires grinding over the crushec
rock driveway, then fading into the distance as it was driver
away. A second later, Demetrio came into the house anc
closed the front door behind him. "Where are you, princess?"

"In the salon," she said.

He strode to where she stood by the fireplace, swept her into a fierce hug and covered her lips with his. Once upon a time, she'd have sold her soul for such a kiss. Would have surrendered without a second thought to the physical hunger he so easily aroused in her. But today, her mind retained control, summarizing the cause of her mental disarray with such stark clarity that she pulled away from him and wiped the back of her hand across her mouth.

The expression in his beautiful blue eyes suddenly veiled, he released her and gestured to the oyster-white leather sofa. "Shall we sit down?"

"I prefer to stand."

"What about something to drink then? Coffee, perhaps?"

"Nothing, thank you," she said, and all too aware that proximity spelled danger where he was concerned, stepped well out of his reach. His smile, a casual brush of his hand against hers, the merest whiff of his aftershave, were just too lethally seductive.

A trace of annoyance crossed his face. "I assure you I don't bite, Natalie. It's quite safe for you to let down your guard."

"That remains to be seen," she said stiffly. "You're so obviously not the man I thought you were that I feel as if I'm facing a stranger. Who are you really, and what are you all about?"

He rocked lightly on the balls of his feet and shoved his hands in his pockets. No sign of generic blue jeans and T-shirt today, she noticed. Instead he wore black loafers, black trousers and a black and white striped shirt with the sleeves rolled halfway up his forearms to reveal a slim gold watch. Casual, classy and very, very expensive.

"Who do you think I am, Natalie?" he asked coolly.

"After your performance last night, I haven't the faintest idea."

"Then let me tell you. I'm exactly the man I've always been and you've always known. Same book, different cover, that's all."

"How can you stand there and expect me to swallow that? You willfully misled me into believing you were…" She lapsed into silence, so much at a loss to come up with something appropriate but tactful that she wished she could just let rip with the kind of crude basics he'd been known to resort to at times.

He wasted no time helping her out. "The ignorant clod next door, barely able to scrape together enough money to knock himself out fixing up a house he had no business owning in the first place?" he supplied harshly. "*Dio,* princess, how come you waited until now to let me in on the fact that you think just like everyone else around here?"

"Don't you dare try to make this my fault!" she retorted. "And don't go putting words in my mouth. I've never been anything but straightforward with you, which is a damn sight more than can be said about the way you've treated me!"

"My, my, such language! What would your grandmama say, if she heard—although, after last night, I suspect it would take a lot more than you could ever throw at her to knock her chair off its rockers." He shook his head, his mouth turning up in a wry smile. "You've gotta love a woman of her stature having the guts to come out and admit in front of her cronies that she's been wrong about the neighborhood scourge."

"Whatever else her faults, my grandmother has never been afraid of the truth—and nor am I."

"Are you suggesting that I am?"

"I'm saying there's something dark and bitter and *twisted* about a man who hides his strengths and accomplishments, and lets people think he has nothing."

"So you're ticked off that I thumbed my nose at your grandmother's society friends. Is that it?"

"No! I'm ticked off because you thumbed your nose at *me*. After all we've shared, I deserved better than that! I was sick with worry about you last night, wondering how you'd handle yourself in that crowd—"

"Nice to know you had so much faith in me!"

"Well, what else do you expect, when you show up wearing that suit, and that shirt and tie? Good grief, didn't you know the kind of impression you gave? Even I was shocked! You looked like—"

She didn't say a *Bertoluzzi*. She didn't have to. "I thought you were smart enough not to be taken in by appearances, Natalie," he said silkily. "Just goes to show how wrong a guy can be when he lets sex enter the picture and cloud his mind."

"This is about a lot more than sex, Demetrio. Once again, I trusted you, and you lied to me."

"Keeping my private life private hardly constitutes lying—"

"It doesn't add up to being open and aboveboard, either! Why couldn't you just have confided everything to me? It's not as if you had anything to be ashamed of!"

"I was tempted, more than once," he practically sneered. "But you were having such a good time playing Lady Bountiful to the miserable bum next door that I hated to spoil your fun."

She could hardly believe what she was hearing. "Is that why you waited until last night to show your true colors? To punish me and watch me squirm for a sin which, by the way, I never even committed?"

"Don't worry about it, princess," he said witheringly. "If I scared you into wetting your pants, nobody noticed. You handled yourself beautifully. To the manner born, as they say."

"You made a fool of me the same way that you made a fool of everyone else, and they all knew it!"

"That's not how your grandmother saw it. I think she quite enjoyed the show."

"Because she's a player, just like you. But that's not how I want to be—and I don't want to be married to someone like that, either!"

He looked around, acting mystified. "Did someone in here propose, and I missed it?"

She recoiled as if he'd delivered an open-handed slap to her face. "Obviously not—but it does leave me wondering why you've bothered me with, these last few months. Exactly what was I to you, Demetrio? A sexual trophy? Someone you could brag to your friends about? *Guess what, I got an American heiress between the sheets, and she didn't even know I'm a millionaire?*"

He looked away, shook his head, and gave that amused little smile that really wasn't amused at all. "You really do have a low opinion of me, don't you, Natalie?"

"If that were true, I'd never have fallen in love with you!"

"You didn't fall in love with me. You fell in love with the idea of a bad-boy hero," he said cuttingly. "I was something different from the pantywaists with whom you and your select little clique of women friends usually associate. I got my hands dirty, then dared to put them on you. Drove a ratty old truck, owned a ratty old dog, screwed you in a ratty old bed." He opened his eyes so wide in a parody of horror that his lashes sprayed out like the petals of some exotic black daisy, and drew out his next remark in a long, quivering falsetto. "'Oh, Matilda, you'll never believe what happened to me! I got laid by the mob!'"

"Shut up!" she cried, hard-pressed not to slap him. "You're being ridiculous!"

"I am?" He stalked toward her, one lethal step at a time. "Aw, come on, Natalie honey, admit it. The thought of being such a naughty girl, doing such naughty things with such a bad, bad man, really turned you on."

"You're wrong. Just because I was sexually naive when we met doesn't make me an idiot." She spoke forcefully enough, but she couldn't quite look him in the eye, because she was afraid there might be a grain of truth in his accusation. Hadn't her first impression of him been that she'd never before come across such a heady combination of danger and sexual magnetism?

He let out a hoot of disbelieving laughter and continued to stalk her, exuding such an air of menace that she shrank away, searching for an avenue of escape.

"Look at me, Natalie!" he roared, backing her against the piano and towering over her. "Stop turning your face away from truths you don't like. See me for who I am, not for what I wear, or what I own, or what you think I should be!"

"How do you expect me to do that, when I don't *know* what kind of man you really you are, and you've never bothered to tell me?" she cried.

As swiftly as his anger had arisen, it died. He blew out a huge sigh, and gave a slow, weary blink. "Because I never thought I had to tell you anything. I thought it was enough to show you. I guess I was wrong."

"I'm afraid you were," she said, her voice breaking. "We all have a past, Demetrio. It's what shapes the people we are today. But you hid all that from me, and showed me only what you wanted me to see. To my way of thinking, that's willful deceit."

He eyed her for the longest time, then gave a weary shrug. "You want the fine print? Okay, here it is."

He flung himself down on the couch and sat a moment, collecting his thoughts, then began.

"Seventeen years ago, when I was exactly half my present age, I left this house and set out to prove myself. I was an ambitious kid, and headed first to Naples, a city I knew well. I was sure I could make something good of my life, but when honest effort didn't bring me the rewards I thought I deserved, I found another way to satisfy my craving for success."

"What kind of way?" she inquired nervously, choosing to sit at the other end of the sofa, as far as away from him as possible, and tucking her knees against her chest as if to ward off a blow.

"A life of crime, princess," he said bluntly. "What is it they say, that you can take a boy out of the country, but you can't take the country out of the boy? That's how it was with me. My grandfather's blood ran in my veins, and he'd taught me well. By the time I turned nineteen, I'd had more close calls with the long arm of the law than I cared to count, and not a single friend worth naming."

"Did you end up in prison?"

"Not quite. I came home again, destitute and disillusioned." He slouched lower on the cushions, his gaze hooded.

"And then?" she prompted gently.

"Big mistake!" he said. "My grandfather was up to his eyeballs in underworld dealings and had run afoul of a rival gang. Living with the threat of retaliation put my grandmother in fear for her life. On top of that, the neighborhood didn't exactly rush to roll out the welcome mat at my return.

"Not long after that, my grandfather's luck ran out. Betrayed from within his own organization, Ovidio Bertoluzzi was arrested and sentenced to a twenty-year prison term."

"Oh, Demetrio, how awful for you!"

He stared through the open French doors to the wide expanse of deep blue sky, but he didn't really see it. His eyes were focused on a different time, and just how much he'd suffered because of it, was written in the bleakness of his gaze and the lines suddenly bracketing his mouth.

"Not for me. I was glad to see the back of him. But the shame broke my grandmother's spirit. That same year, on a cold gray morning in late November, she died in the room directly above the one you're sitting in now."

Natalie's heart contracted with pity, for him and for his grandmother. She ached to put her arms around him and tell him how desperately sorry she was, but he was too isolated in grief to be reached, and the most she could do was lean over and touch his arm in silent sympathy.

He promptly shifted out of reach. "The night before, I sat by her bed, held her hand and begged God not to take away the only person I'd ever loved—or who'd loved me. God didn't listen, but He lent her enough strength to open her eyes one last time and say, 'Demetrio, in you I see the man I hoped your father would be. I see determination and intelligence and great beauty of soul, but I fear that you inherited the same weakness that left him dead in the gutter at thirty-one. Promise me you'll fight this curse which plagues the men of my family, and rise above it. Please, Demetrio, child of my heart, promise me you'll be the best that you can be, and never give up on yourself or your dreams.'"

Natalie brushed a surreptitious finger against the tear beading her cheek. How deeply that sweet and gentle lady must have suffered in her lifetime, to harbor such fear for a child she loved so unselfishly.

"Her voice wasn't much more than a papery whisper by then," Demetrio continued, "and I had to bend close to hear. But her words emblazoned themselves in my mind. Robbed of the one person who'd really mattered to me, I took a long, hard look at what I'd become—discontented, resentful, shiftless—and vowed I'd honor her memory by making something of myself, or die trying."

"And you did!" No point being furtive about the tears

now. They streamed down her face in torrents. "You don't have to explain any further, Demetrio. I understand now what last night—"

He cut her off as if he hadn't heard a word she said. "Within the week, I took all those things she treasured most, hid them in storage, left what remained for the enjoyment of the grandfather I hoped never to see again and visited her one last time. 'I will make you proud, Nonna,' I told her, laying a wreath of laurel and rosemary on her grave. 'I promise I will not disappoint you again.'"

He looked at Natalie then, his gaze once more centered on the present. "I never have, and I never will."

"I believe you," she said earnestly, "and I'm so sorry I didn't give you—"

"I'm not finished," he snapped, his words slicing the atmosphere, and the laser beam of his eyes skewering her with such a look of cold indifference that she cringed.

"I made my way to Milan and found work on a construction crew. By day, I learned the tricks of the building trade. At night, I worked as a waiter. Within a year, I'd saved enough to upgrade my education and study part-time at the university. Several months later, a law firm in Naples traced me through the construction company and told me my grandfather had died in jail. As the sole surviving family member, I inherited everything. Overnight, I went from living just above poverty level to owning this villa, and a substantial cache of money whose origins didn't bear close inspection."

She couldn't help interrupting again. Spreading her hands to encompass the restored villa and grounds, she asked, "Is that how you were able to afford all this?"

He spared her another searing glance, this one loaded with contempt. "Perhaps you didn't hear me the first time, so I'll say it again. I honored my promise to my grandmother."

"So you refused the money?"

"Keeping my word didn't make me fool enough to look a gift horse in the mouth, even if I didn't much like its pedigree! That money paid my way through a three-year course in Political Science, and a specialized degree in Economics and International Finance at the University of Milan, plus the Princeton MBA that set you all back on your heels, last night."

He laughed bitterly. "I took particular pleasure in turning such ill-gotten gains into something worthwhile, if only because I knew it would have my grandfather spinning in his grave."

"And the traveling?"

"He paid for that, too—something else he'd have found a colossal waste. But there's more to living well than having a string of letters behind your name, and believe it or not, princess, you don't have to be born with a silver spoon in your mouth to acquire a little culture.

"It took me longer than most, perhaps, but I'm a quick study when I put my mind to something. You might have noticed that I didn't drag my knuckles across the floor when I came into your grandmother's home last night, and I was able to converse at the dinner table without grunting."

"That remark is *so* uncalled-for, Demetrio, and you know it!" she protested.

He rolled his eyes. "It's a bit late in the game to claim your undying faith in me."

Exasperated, she rolled hers in perfect imitation. "First of all, I've never seen this as a game. And second, I've never doubted that, at heart, you're basically as decent a man as any I've ever met."

"You're trying too hard to spare my feelings, princess," he said shortly. "Not ten minutes ago, you accused me of not being the man you thought I was. What if you were right? What if the legacy of bloodshed and crime is so deeply ingrained in my genetic makeup that I can't shed it, no matter how hard I try to pass myself off as respectable?"

"It's not. I'd know if it were."

"You don't know squat about how the other half lives. You have no idea of the depths of degradation to which a man can sink."

"Be quiet! This time, I'm the one that's not finished!" she snapped. "Belittle me all you like, Demetrio Bertoluzzi, but I've had a fair bit of experience at reading people myself, and I didn't save my virginity all this time just to hand it over to an underworld thug—and you know very well that you're the only man I've ever slept with."

"Forgive me for wondering why."

"You already know why, but I'm not too proud to tell you again. I'm in love with you! Why else was I ready to rip out the throat of anyone who said a wrong word to you, last night? I wanted to shield you from slights—from being hurt."

"Well, here's a news flash, Natalie," he informed her stonily. "I don't need you to defend me. I'm not in the habit of hiding behind a woman's skirts, and I'm not looking for another mother."

Painfully stung, she said, "My mistake—one of many, it seems." She heard the tears in her voice and knew he heard them, too. Furious at the weakness she couldn't control, she spat, "You know what, Demetrio? I've had it with you! You can rot in hell, for all I care. You'll probably feel right at home there."

"Are you done?"

"Yes," she said. "I'm done."

"Then I suggest you go home to your grandmother, and leave me to get on with my imperfect life, the best way I know how. Better yet, go back to the U.S. and forget you ever met me."

She bit down so hard on the inside of her cheek that she could taste blood. Her throat ached, and that distant chiming which only she could hear signaled the splintering of her heart into a million tiny pieces.

Rallying her pride, she eased herself off the couch and said with quiet dignity, "I can't imagine there's anything left to say after that. It would seem we're both finished—with each other, and with any idea I nurtured that there might one day have been an 'us.'"

Then she walked away, concentrating only on putting one foot in front of the other and disappearing from his sight, before she gave in to the tears blinding her.

For the rest of the day, he behaved like the damned fool he almost certainly was, and drank himself into oblivion. The next morning, he woke up on the floor in his bedroom with no memory of staggering upstairs, not sure if the hammers pounding the inside of his skull were the result of his having fallen out of bed in the middle of the night, or because he was nursing one mother of a hangover.

A very long shower, aspirin and a pot of coffee helped his headache, but did nothing to ease the pain in his heart. Recognizing that he could name a dozen women who'd be happy to warm his bed, offered no comfort. Nor did the knowledge that the social circles in which he now moved had never once questioned the whys and wherefores of his accomplishments, but had simply accepted him as a man who bore the invisible trappings of success as easily as he wore his custom-tailored suits.

It should be enough, and it wasn't. Without Natalie in his life, nothing mattered, not even the company he'd built from the ground up and which now ranked among the best in its field throughout Italy.

"Your old man's an idiot," he informed Pippo, who opened one eye just long to signal his agreement, then went back to sleep in the corner of her kitchen.

Her kitchen.

He blinked, wondering when he'd stopped thinking of the house as his project, and started making it over into a place where Natalie would want to live?

The first time they made love? When he saw the dirt under her fingernails after she'd weeded his grandmother's rose bed? The time Pippo left muddy pawprints all over her white skirt, and she'd laughed and said that's why washing machines had been invented? Or had it all started the day she arrived at her grandmother's and saw him watching her from the roof?

He had no answers but one: falling in love with her had been easy, but falling out was beyond him. Which left him with only one course of action.

"You just missed her," Barbara Wade told him, when he phoned. "I'm very sorry, Mr. Bertoluzzi, but she's decided to cut short her holiday and go back home. My chauffeur's driving her to Naples as we speak."

"I'm afraid I can't allow that to happen," he said. "I intend to marry your granddaughter, and I don't believe in long engagements or long-distance relationships. I want her here with me."

"Then I suggest you stop wasting time talking to me and try telling her that. Samuele is a very circumspect driver and has only a ten-minute head start. If you hurry, you'll catch him long before he reaches the city. Would you like to use one of my cars? I don't imagine your truck's capable of getting the job done."

"Thank you, Signora Wade, but I have other transportation."

"Then keep your eye out for a black Mercedes, and good luck. I await my granddaughter's return with great anticipation."

CHAPTER THIRTEEN

ALTHOUGH a numb sort of disbelief shielded her from the ugliness of that last meeting with Demetrio, Natalie knew she couldn't afford to remain in Italy. The temptation to run next door and beg him to give them another chance was too acute, and her pride wouldn't stand for that.

Leaving was so painful, she didn't know how she held herself together, and once wrapped in the privacy of her grandmother's air-conditioned Mercedes limousine, with the chimneys of Villa Delfina sliding out of view behind the trees, Natalie fell apart.

Memories of her too-brief summer of love swamped her. Of the day she'd arrived in Amalfi, and caught Demetrio watching her from his rooftop. Of the afternoon he'd stopped to give her a lift home, and she'd ridden in his battered old truck, an underfed, abandoned puppy in her lap. Of the many times they'd flung themselves down in the long, sweet grass in his garden, and laughed together, over Pippo, or something one of them had said, or for no reason at all but that they were together and life was good.

She remembered his touch, his kiss, the fierce blue fire in his eyes just before he climaxed. The endearments he'd murmured, the words falling from his lips in a stream of liquid, lyrical Italian.

They should have had forever. A lifetime of passion-filled nights, laughter-filled days. Quiet times drenched in peace and contentment, and yes, occasional disagreements that made the rafters ring, because that's what real life was all about. They should have had babies...

She choked on a sob, awash in grief for what might have been, and tried to divert it by reminding herself of what was.

Right from the start, she had given him her all. It was the only way she knew how to love. And right from the start, he'd held a part of himself back. He couldn't help it. It was as much a part of his genetic makeup as the color of his eyes.

Perhaps some women could live with that, but she wasn't one of them. Sooner or later, it would have undermined their relationship. Better it should happen now while they were both free to move on, than later when they might have been married, with children.

Miserably she rested her head against the back of her seat and closed her eyes, willing herself to sink into the merciful escape of sleep.

It wasn't to be. The blast of a horn, from a car following too close behind, penetrated the snug interior of the Mercedes, scattering the mists closing in on her mind and jolting her to attention.

"Maniac!" Samuele mouthed, glancing in his rearview mirror.

The horn sounded again, three strident, imperative honks, and from the corner of her eye she saw the bright red hood of a low-slung Ferrari zoom up on the left. But instead of passing, as he could easily have done, the driver kept pace with the Mercedes in a dangerous duet of speed.

"Imbecile!" Samuele roared, shaking his fist as a fourth prolonged cacophony split the air. "Road hog! Where are the police when you need them?"

"I think he's trying to tell you to pull over," Natalie said, rolling down her window for a better view, even though all she could see was the roof of the other vehicle. "Maybe he i the police and he's in a ghost car."

"More likely he is a lunatic, *signorina*."

When the Ferrari suddenly zipped in front of the Mercedes, then slammed on its brakes, forcing Samuele to do the same, she began to think he was right. Only by the grace of God and Samuele's skill did the big limo avoid plowing into the rear of the smaller car and skid to a stop on the shoulder of the road instead.

The driver was out of the Ferrari in a flash and racing toward the Mercedes. Before Samuele had the presence of mind to activate the automatic window controls, the man reached through the one Natalie had opened, unlocked her door and leaped onto the backseat next to her.

She had a brief, dazed image of dark hair in disarray, and light blue eyes in a sun-bronzed face, before his arms swept around her and crushed her to him. His voice, sinful as dark chocolate laced with honeyed brandy, rumbled from the depths of his chest, fractured with emotion.

"Thank God I caught up with you in time, princess," he said.

It took several minutes for Demetrio to convince Samuele that she was in no danger of being kidnapped and that it was perfectly all right for him to transfer her from the Mercedes to the Ferrari. Even then, Samuele insisted on using the car phone to verify matters with her grandmother.

Throughout, Natalie behaved with wooden composure. She fastened her seat belt, and sat with her hands folded in her lap and her feet neatly aligned next to each other, and stared through the windshield, and watched the scenery flash by as the Ferrari sped along the highway…and waited for the dream to end and reality to come crashing back.

When it didn't, when instead Demetrio turned in at the gates of Villa Delfina and brought the car to a stop at the foot of the front steps, and said, "We're home, princess," and she had every reason in the world to rejoice, she fell apart again.

She put her face in her hands and burst into noisy tears. They gushed from her eyes in torrents as if they'd never stop. Her sobs filled the car, floated out to invade the gardens. She tried to say she was sorry, that she didn't know why she was being so foolish, that she really was perfectly all right, and succeeded only in choking out a mangled, unintelligible jumble of sound that made no sense at all.

Demetrio's arms came around her again, gently this time. He cushioned her head against his shoulder and stroked her hair and let her cry. He was warm and strong and real. She could feel his breath against her hair, hear his heart's steady, reassuring beat.

A long time passed before the dark cloud of shock which had held her in such a suffocating grip lifted, with nothing to show for it but her occasional ragged hiccup and a big wet spot on his shirt.

"You don't happen to have a brown paper bag in this car, do you?" she asked shakily, pulling away from him and scrubbing at her face.

"Afraid not, my darling. Why do you ask?"

She'd never been one of those women who could cry prettily. "I need something to stick my head in. I can just imagine how I must look—like a mashed tomato, probably."

He took the tail of his shirt and tenderly wiped her face. "But I'm Italian, remember? I like tomatoes. They're a staple part of my diet. I can't imagine going a single day without them."

She almost managed a smile. "I bet you say that to all your women."

"No, princess," he said soberly, his eyes scouring her face, his fingers gentle at her jaw. "Just to you. Because you're the *only* woman in my life, and if you leave me again, it won't be worth a plugged nickel."

"I never wanted to leave," she said. "I just couldn't bear to stay, thinking it was over between us."

"It will never be over."

"Are you sure?"

"I'm sure," he said, right before he kissed her with desperate, driving hunger.

Long minutes later, he said, "Will you come inside the house and let me explain myself?"

"Of course I will." She unlatched her seat belt. Not until he came around to open her door and help her out of the low-slung Ferrari did it occur to her to ask, "Where's your old truck, and whose car is this?"

"The old truck's received an honorable discharge. The car's mine."

A soft gurgle escaped her—real laughter this time. "I should have guessed. What real, honest-to-God Italian doesn't own at least one red Ferrari?"

"Actually," he said, bending down to whisper in her ear, "I have a Lamborghini, too, but it's not red."

She pulled away, and tugged her linen jacket and skirt into place—the same linen jacket and skirt she'd worn the day she arrived at her grandmother's, half a lifetime ago. "This is all too much to take in. I think you'd better get started on those explanations."

"May I suggest we invite your grandmother to join us? When we spoke on the phone this morning, I mentioned a few things to her which she's probably having some difficulty dealing with. It might ease her mind to hear what I'm about to tell you."

Beyond being surprised by anything at that point, she agreed. When Barbara arrived, he ushered her into the salon, waited until she'd hugged Natalie and taken a seat next to her on the couch, then began.

"You know, of course, that I've deliberately misrepresented myself to you since the day I came back here, and that I'm not quite the dubious individual I let you think I was, but I realize there's still much you need to learn about me before I can ask your forgiveness, or expect you to accept me without reservation."

"Then get on with it, young man," her grandmother said, "and stop keeping us in suspense."

"Very well." He took a turn around the room and stopped before an oil painting of a woman in her early forties, newly hung above the fireplace since Natalie had last been there. She had on a burgundy evening gown cut along classical lines, in some rich fabric that might have been velvet, and wore her dark hair in a chignon. A triple strand of pearls hung around her long, graceful neck, ending in a pendant formed by a cluster of diamonds. The same motif showed in her earrings.

Natalie recognized her, of course. Although still beautiful, the haunting sadness so evident in her wedding photograph was diminished now by strength that betrayed a spine of steel beneath the elegant gown. Yet a world of sweetness glimmered behind in her smile, and a wealth of wisdom shone in her eyes.

"This is a portrait of my grandmother," Demetrio said.

Barbara nodded. "Yes. I remember her well. She was a lady."

"She was my inspiration," he replied. "Because of her, I embarked on a long and arduous journey from where I was at the time of her death, to where I stand today. I was twenty-eight when I returned to Italy after Princeton, and I settled in Milan because I'd started out there, working in construction."

"Small wonder you were so capable when it came to fixing up this house," Barbara observed.

"That, not my education, is what had made a man of me, and I turned to it again, opening my own small renovation company with a crew of five. I borrowed the money to buy an old, run-down villa on a prime lot next to a park not far from the tourist section of town, and turned it into a boutique hotel. A risky gamble, others in my line of work warned me, but it paid off handsomely. Since then, I've expanded considerably, with branches in Firenze and Genoa." He looked directly at Natalie, and permitted himself a smile. "And very recently, as far south as the Amalfi coast."

"Those dark green vans and trucks with the name painted on the side in gold—*Emerenzia Costruzione*, wasn't it?—they were yours!" she exclaimed.

"That's right. Emerenzia was my grandmother's middle name." He paused and touched the frame holding her portrait, in silent acknowledgment of the woman who, as he'd so aptly put it, had been his inspiration. "For a while, success brought its own reward. I could afford luxury cars, a penthouse in the high rent district of the city, a ski lodge in the Alps, an apartment in Venice."

Then turning, he addressed his next remark to Barbara. "I mention this not to impress you with how much money I make, *signora,* but to alleviate any concern you might have that I'm looking to take advantage of Natalie's wealth."

"The thought did cross my mind at one point," she admitted. "But please go on with your story."

"After a while, a certain malaise set in. I realized there was one thing money couldn't buy: proving myself to those who'd known me when I was nothing, and had nothing, and revealing myself as the one Bertoluzzi heir who'd declined to continue the legacy of his forefathers. I could have taken the easy way out and completely reinvented myself. Changed my name, sold this villa, married well and started a new dynasty in Milan."

Again, he glanced at the portrait. "But to do so would have meant denying the one person who'd believed in me, and that I would not do. My grandmother had enabled me to rise to my present level of success. The least I could do in return was erase the shame that sent her to her grave. So I came back to the place she'd loved more than anywhere else on earth and set about returning it to its former glory."

"But you didn't reveal yourself to us at all," Barbara pointed out. "You chose instead to camouflage who you've become, and I fail to understand the reason for it. What did you hope to gain by dressing like a common—and dare I add, unskilled—laborer, driving around in that pathetic wreck of a vehicle? Why not show up as the man you really are, and avoid the kind of suspicion and mistrust you encouraged with your bizarre behavior?"

He shook his head, and smiled. "And what would have been your immediate assumption, Signora Wade, had I arrived apparently as well able to afford the task I'd set myself, just as my grandfather was always able to afford whatever he decided he had to have?"

She opened her mouth to reply, then closed it again as the import of his question hit home.

"Exactly," he said. "The suspicion and mistrust would have doubled. Not only that, there was another reason for the way I went about things. I needed to prove I was capable of taking on a difficult task and accomplishing it with honest work and dedicated effort—not just to you and others living close by, but to myself. It was my gift to my grandmother. A repayment of the debt I owed her, if you like. I believe I have achieved that goal."

"I believe it, too," Natalie said, emotions churning thick in her breast. "I believe in you, Demetrio."

"And I believe I was right in saying that there's more to you than meets the eye," her grandmother put in. "You are a quite remarkable young man, Demetrio Bertoluzzi."

He held up his hand. "There's more," he said, and focused his attention on Natalie again. "Not long ago, you accused me of lying to you, and you were right to do so. I lied for the better part of two months."

A chill overtook the warmth in her heart. Dreading how he might reply, she said, "Why, Demetrio? I don't understand."

"Because I was approached by the police in Positano, and asked to cooperate in bringing down a man whose greed and corruption have caused a lot of misery in these parts and who, left unchecked, would have continued to wreak havoc. You know who I'm talking about, princess. Guido Cattanasca."

"*That* abominable creature?" her grandmother exploded contemptuously. "It's about time someone put a stop to his shenanigans. But I don't see why the police had to involve you."

"He wanted to buy this property because he'd bribed or coerced those in authority to effect a change in zoning bylaws that would permit him to demolish the house and build a multi-residence complex on this land."

"Good *grief!*" Barbara looked to be on the verge of a stroke.

"I see I don't have to spell out the devastating impact such a development would have had on you and our other neighbors," Demetrio observed dryly. "It was to put a stop to that, and all the other crooked deals in which he's involved, that I agreed to go along with the police."

He switched his attention to Natalie again. "I'm deeply sorry that, as part of my confidentiality agreement with them, and also to shield you from exposure to Cattanasca, I had to lie to you. I promise you now that I will never deceive or disappoint you, ever again."

"Don't you dare apologize," she said, tremulous with relief. "You're perfect just as you are."

"Oh, princess," he replied, his voice suspiciously hoarse, "I'm a long way from perfect."

"How can you be? You're my hero."

"Some hero! Heroes don't let pride make them risk losing the one person in the world who matters more to them than anything or anyone else in the world."

"Say what you like, Demetrio," she argued. "You're still my kind of hero, whether you like it, or not."

He cleared his throat and brushed a hand over his eyes. "Then perhaps you'll give serious consideration to the only thing left I have to say."

"Oops!" Her grandmother jumped up from the couch. "This is where I make myself scarce. Where's your wine cellar, Demetrio?"

"Next to the walk-in pantry in the kitchen," he said. "Go down the hall next to the staircase and—"

She patted his hand before heading out of the room. "I'll find it, darling. You've got bigger things to worry about than my getting lost."

"What's she talking about?" Natalie inquired nervously, as Barbara's footsteps faded away. "What kind of bigger things, and why are you worried about them?"

"Because I'm not sure if you'll give me the answer I'm hoping for." He got up from his chair and dropped to one knee in front of her. "I haven't said this before, because there were other matters that needed straightening out first, but I'm free now to tell you that I love you with everything I am, Natalie. I cannot imagine not having you by my side. I want you to share your life with me, make a home, bear my children."

He stopped just long enough to pull a small velvet box from his pocket and snap it open to reveal an emerald-cut diamond solitaire mounted in platinum. "I know you have plans to take over from your grandmother at Wade International one day, and I'd never ask you to give those up. But I am asking you to marry me, princess."

"Oh!" She bit down hard on her lower lip and welcomed the pain because it told her she wasn't dreaming. The diamond turned into a blinding swirl of brilliant light. She wouldn't have thought she had any tears left to shed, but they came anyway, flavored with joy this time. "And I'm accepting," she said. "I'll be proud to marry you, Demetrio, and be the mother of your children. I'll be proud for the world to know me as your wife, Mrs. Demetrio Bertoluzzi."

He rose and pulled her into his arms. "I promise you'll never regret it, my love."

"Stop talking," she begged, "and just kiss me."

He did. At great and ardent length. "And that," he murmured, "is just for starters. The best is yet to come."

"I take it," her grandmother said, parading into the room at that point with Pippo bringing up the rear, and setting a tray down on a table out of his reach, "that I made the right choice when I opened this very fine bottle of champagne?"

"Indeed you did," Demetrio said, anchoring Natalie to him with an arm around her waist. "Your granddaughter has agreed to become my wife."

"Oh dear! Then I suppose that means you'll be taking her to live in Milan."

"I have no such intention, Signora. This house should be filled with love, and the laughter of children—with *our* children. I plan to open another branch of my company in the area." He smiled. "After all, with Cattanasca out of business, there's room for a legitimate operation to take over and put right some of the damage he's caused. But more than that, I know what it's like to be separated from the person who's been a driving influence in your life, and I would never ask Natalie to give up her close ties to you, just because she happens to be married to me. I hope that's enough for you to give us your blessing, Signora Wade."

"You know it is," she said. "And Demetrio, my friends call me Barbara. Since you're about to join the family, I'd consider it a very great honor if you'd do the same. And now let's get to the champagne. I wish to make a toast."

She lifted her glass. "To you, my darling Natalie, for seeing the gold in this man that I, with all my vast experience, failed to detect. And to you, Demetrio, for the risks you've taken to bring us to this day. May your life together be long and filled with happiness."

Natalie looked at him over the rim of her glass and found herself trapped in his gaze. He smiled, and lowered his lashes in a long, slow wink that promised all that, and much, much more.

THE SULTAN'S
VIRGIN BRIDE
by Sarah Morgan

Men who can't be tamed...or so they think!

Meet the guy who breaks the rules to get exactly
what he wants, because he is...

HARD-EDGED & HANDSOME

He's the man who's impossible to resist.

RICH & RAKISH

He's got everything—and needs nobody...
until he meets one woman.

He's RUTHLESS!

In his pursuit of passion; in his world the winner takes all!

Billionaire Sebastian Armstrong thinks he knows his
housekeeper inside out. But beneath Emily's plain-Jane
workday exterior there's a passionate woman trying to
forget she's fallen in love with her handsome boss.

THE RUTHLESS
MARRIAGE PROPOSAL
by Miranda Lee

On sale June 2007.

REQUEST YOUR FREE BOOKS!

HARLEQUIN® *Presents*~

PASSION GUARANTEED SEDUCTION

2 FREE NOVELS PLUS 2 FREE GIFTS!

YES! Please send me 2 FREE Harlequin Presents® novels and my 2 FREE gifts. After receiving them, if I don't wish to receive any more books, I can return the shipping statement marked "cancel." If I don't cancel, I will receive 6 brand-new novels every month and be billed just $3.80 per book in the U.S., or $4.47 per book in Canada, plus 25¢ shipping and handling per book and applicable taxes, if any*. That's a savings of close to 15% off the cover price! I understand that accepting the 2 free books and gifts places me under no obligation to buy anything. I can always return a shipment and cancel at any time. Even if I never buy another book from Harlequin, the two free books and gifts are mine to keep forever.

106 HDN EEXK 306 HDN EEXV

Name _____ (PLEASE PRINT)

Address _____ Apt. #

City _____ State/Prov. _____ Zip/Postal Code

Signature (if under 18, a parent or guardian must sign)

Mail to the Harlequin Reader Service®:

IN U.S.A.: P.O. Box 1867, Buffalo, NY 14240-1867
IN CANADA: P.O. Box 609, Fort Erie, Ontario L2A 5X3

Not valid to current Harlequin Presents subscribers.

Want to try two free books from another line?
Call 1-800-873-8635 or visit www.morefreebooks.com.

* Terms and prices subject to change without notice. NY residents add applicable sales tax. Canadian residents will be charged applicable provincial taxes and GST. This offer is limited to one order per household. All orders subject to approval. Credit or debit balances in a customer's account(s) may be offset by any other outstanding balance owed by or to the customer. Please allow 4 to 6 weeks for delivery.

Your Privacy: Harlequin is committed to protecting your privacy. Our Privacy Policy is available online at www.eHarlequin.com or upon request from the Reader Service. From time to time we make our lists of customers available to reputable firms who may have a product or service of interest to you. If you would prefer we not share your name and address, please check here. ☐

HP07

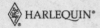